Sweet Tomorrows

HONEYSUCKLE TEXAS ★ BOOK 6

CHRIS KENISTON

Indie House Publishing

This book is a work of fiction. Names, characters, places and incidents are the product of the author's imagination or are used fictionally. Any resemblance to actual events, locales, or persons, living or dead, is coincidental.

Copyright 2025 Christine Baena
Print Edition

Indie House Publishing

MORE BOOKS
By Chris Keniston

Honeysuckle Texas
Sweet Beginnings
Sweet Surprise
Sweet Temptation
Sweet Deal
Sweet Obsession
Sweet Tomorrows
Sweet Redemption

The Billionaire Barons of Texas
Just One Date
Just One Spark
Just One Dance
Just One Take
Just One Taste
Just One Shot
Just One Chance
Just One Mistake
Just One Family
Just One Rodeo
Just One Surprise
Just One Look

Hart Land Lakeside Inn
Heather
Lily
Violet
Iris
Hyacinth
Rose
Calytrix
Zinnia

Poppy
Picture Perfect

Farraday Country
Adam
Brooks
Connor
Declan
Ethan
Finn
Grace
Hannah
Ian
Jamison
Keeping Eileen
Loving Chloe
Morgan
Neil
Owen
Paxton
Quinn

Honeymoon Series
Honeymoon for One
Honeymoon for Three
Honeymoon for Four
Honeymoon for Five
Honeymoon for Six
Honeymoon for Seven

Aloha Romance Series:
Aloha Texas
Almost Paradise
Mai Tai Marriage
Dive Into You
Look of Love
Love by Design
Love Walks In
Shell Game
Flirting with Paradise

Fake Dating the SEAL

Surf's Up Flirts:
(Aloha Series Companions)
Shall We Dance
Love on Tap
Head Over Heels
Perfect Match
Just One Kiss
It Had to Be You
Cat's Meow

CHAPTER ONE

The familiar scent of old leather, paper, and their father's cologne should have felt like coming home. Instead, leaning against the doorframe of the study, to Kade Sweet it felt like visiting a museum of a life that was no longer his. The chaotic, sprawling family of his youth had now settled into smaller, tighter pairings of two. Carson's hand rested on Jess's knee, an easy, possessive gesture. Across the room, Preston murmured something to Sarah Sue, and the private smile they shared was a conversation all its own. Garret and Jackie sat on the floor, their easy affection a comfortable fixture in the room now. Even Rachel and Jim, his free-spirited sister and her childhood-friend-turned-husband, seemed to share a quiet, solid understanding. And then there was Jillian, his youngest sister, radiating a new, confident happiness as she leaned against the rock star who had somehow become her husband.

Kade felt relegated to little more than an observer. A low, contented sigh from his side was his only anchor. Kade looked down at Brady, the big German Shepherd's head resting on his boot. The dog, at least, was a constant.

"All right," Preston's voice cut through the low chatter, pulling Kade's attention from his thoughts to the laptop open on their father's desk. "Time for the state of the union."

A collective settling fell over the room. This was the new normal—the family pow-wow, the mission briefing for the ongoing campaign to save the Sweet Ranch.

"Good news first," Preston continued, a rare, unforced smile touching his lips. "Thanks to the initial payments and everyone's hard work, we're holding the line. The operating budget is stable, if not exactly comfortable. We're meeting the monthly payments."

A collective, quiet sigh of relief went through the room. It wasn't a victory, not yet, but it was a far sight better than the desperate freefall they'd been in when he'd first heard of their not-so-trusted foreman's thievery.

"The real light at the end of the tunnel is still the anniversary payouts," Carson added, his voice steady. "Only a few more months to go and the first anniversary stipend will hit. From there, we can easily pay off the biggest of Dad's loans. Give us some real breathing room."

"In other words, by the time they all roll in, we'll be in the clear?" Garret squeezed his wife's hand.

The plan was working. The insane, beautiful, ridiculous plan had actually worked. Kade felt a surge of pride for his siblings, for the incredible new spouses who had stepped up to join their fight. For the homes they'd created.

Preston lifted his chin to his older brother. "I'm not making any promises yet, but, if all continues to go well, you, brother Kade, may very well be off the hook. We might be able to hold the fort down until the big payments start rolling in."

It was Jillian who turned her gaze on him, a mischievous sparkle in her eyes that he remembered all too well from their childhood. "Of course," she said, her voice laced with theatrical innocence, "now that Blake and I are moving into our own place, the master bedroom will be free again so… if you happened to fall in love in the next few months, it certainly wouldn't hurt the budget."

The room erupted in easy laughter. Kade felt the corner of his own mouth twitch. "Noted." He held back a chuckle, shaking his head. Though lord knows why he was laughing. Perhaps because, for everyone, the guillotine of foreclosure was no longer hanging over their necks.

As the conversation shifted to a brief, if uneventful update on the still-missing Ray and the two ranch hands caught in Wyoming, Kade's mind drifted again. He looked at his brothers, men who were now husbands and fathers, their lives intricately woven into the fabric of this land. He had always defined himself by his service, his duty to his country. It was a clear, honorable path. But for the first time, watching the life his family was building, a life of shared burdens and quiet joys, he questioned his own future. Was a career spent thousands of miles away truly the best thing for him, or for them? What was his legacy beyond a distinguished service record?

The sharp ring of his phone cut through his thoughts, a jarring intrusion from the outside world. He glanced at the caller ID—Sully, his best friend from his unit. Frowning, he pushed off the doorframe. "Excuse me a second."

He stepped into the hallway, the murmur of his family's voices fading behind him. "Sully. What's up?"

"Hey, I was hoping I'd catch you."

Kade smiled despite his exhaustion. Dan "Sully" Sullivan had been in his unit three deployments ago, a solid soldier and an even better friend. "What's all that racket? Where the heck are you?"

"Vegas. That's, uh, actually why I'm calling." Sully's laugh sounded forced. "I'm getting married. Tomorrow night. I know it's short notice, but I need a best man, and you're the only guy I trust not to let me do something completely stupid."

"Tomorrow night? Sully, what the hell—"

"I know how it sounds. But Kade, she's the one. I met her six months ago when I was passing through on leave, and I haven't been able to get her out of my head since. She's got orders for Germany next month. It's now or we wait two years, and I can't wait two years."

Kade closed his eyes, already knowing what his answer would be. Sully had saved his ass more times than he could count. If his friend needed him, he'd be there.

"What time do you need me?"

"Are you serious?" The relief in Sully's voice was palpable. "Man, I owe you big time. Ceremony's at eight. Nothing fancy, just a quick thing at one of the chapels, then we'll hit the town to celebrate."

"Text me the details. And Sullivan—you sure about this?"

"Never been more sure of anything in my life."

A moment later, he walked back into the study, the phone now silent in his hand. Every eye in the room on him.

He ran a hand over his face, a slow grin spreading across his lips. "Well, change of plans. I'm hopping on a flight in the morning."

"What's going on?" Jillian's brow furrowed with concern.

Kade shook his head, the absurdity of it all hitting him. "Sully's getting married. In Vegas. And apparently, I'm the best man."

From Cassidy Barker's side of the blackjack table, the casino floor was a symphony of calculated loss and manufactured joy. The incessant, cheerful chime of a nearby slot machine paying out a minor jackpot was just a percussive accent to the low, steady hum of a hundred simultaneous conversations. Her hands, however, were silent. They moved with a liquid economy of motion that belied the complex mathematics spinning behind her eyes. Shuffle, cut, deal. The rhythm was second nature, a muscle memory so deep it left her mind free to wander. And it always wandered.

Two of hearts to the honeymooners on seat one. A seven to the desperate salesman on three. Face card to the wannabe pro on five, who thinks his sunglasses make him look mysterious instead of like a man who forgot to take out the trash.

Her internal ledger kept a running tally, a silent game she played to stave off the soul-crushing boredom. The count was hot. Not just warm, but sizzling—a high-card-heavy shoe that any decent card counter would be drooling over. The salesman on three should be doubling down, but he was too busy sweating through his shirt to notice. The honeymooners were too caught up in each other to care.

It was this—this constant, whirring calculus—that her

most recent ex had never understood. "You're always in your head," he'd said last week, the final words in a relationship that had fizzled out with less drama than a losing hand. "It's like you're a million miles away."

He wasn't wrong. Most of the time, she *was* a million miles away, calculating what to do with the rest of her life. Something other than this. The problem was, she had no idea what that something else was. A degree? In what? A new city? Which one? For a woman who could track the probability of a ten-point card appearing with ninety-eight percent accuracy, her own future was a complete statistical anomaly.

A bride, judging by the ridiculously new-looking ring on her finger—hesitated, her hand hovering over her two cards. A soft nineteen. The dealer's up-card was a six. Cassidy's mind supplied the odds in a flash.

She caught the young woman's eye for a fraction of a second, giving the slightest, almost imperceptible shake of her head. "Insurance is a sucker's bet, folks," her voice in a low, even monotone, expressed the standard casino line that was, for once, the absolute truth.

The husband nodded, pulling his wife's hand back. "She's right, honey. We stand."

Cassidy played out the hand, flipping her down card to reveal a four. She hit, pulled a nine, and busted. She paid out the table's winnings with a practiced, neutral expression. It was a small act of rebellion, a tiny nudge of the odds in someone else's favor. It was all the control she had here.

Her gaze drifted past the players, over the sea of heads. The casino floor buzzed with its usual Friday night chaos— slot machines continuously chiming, dice clattering, voices rising and falling in waves of excitement and disappointment. After three years, it all blurred into background noise. Just another shift. Just another night of watching people gamble away rent money while she calculated her own odds of getting out of this life. She'd grown up in the foster system, passed between houses like a well-worn deck of cards, learning early that the only person you could ever truly count on was yourself. She had no family photos in her small apartment, no sentimental heirlooms. Just a growing savings account and a vague, persistent ache for roots she'd never had. She wanted more than this transient life, more than the fleeting connections of the casino floor. She just didn't know how to get it.

The pit boss appeared at the edge of her vision, tapping his watch. Shift change. Relief washed over her, cool and immediate. She finished the hand, expertly cleared the table, and pushed a neat stack of chips toward her replacement. "Table's all yours."

"Anything exciting?" The woman slid into the seat.

"Never is." She walked away from the table, the noise of the casino floor already receding. She navigated the endless labyrinth of employee hallways, the scent of industrial cleaner a welcome change from the cloying perfume of the main floor. In the stark, fluorescent light of the locker room, she shed the dealer's uniform and the professional calm that went with it. In her own clothes—jeans and a soft, worn t-shirt—she felt anonymous again. She felt like herself. Whoever that was.

Her phone buzzed with a text from the leasing office. *Reminder: Response needed on lease renewal by Monday.*

For a brief while she'd forgotten that the landlord was raising the rent on her tiny one-bedroom apartment with leaky pipes and noisy neighbors. Three days to decide if she was staying or going. In the last two weeks since she'd gotten notice of the rent increase, she'd looked at a few other apartments, not much cheaper, not much better. She was definitely going to have to make up her mind. Stay or leave. Though she knew what she'd do. What she always did. Stay with the familiar. She'd done enough moving from place to place the first eighteen years of her life, she was tired of packing.

Heading out into the artificial dusk of the casino's shopping promenade, she felt the familiar pull of restlessness. Another night done. Another small deposit made into the escape fund. Maybe tomorrow she'd look at those college brochures again. Maybe she'd finally fill one out. Or maybe she'd just keep doing what she'd always done—surviving one day at a time, waiting for something to change while knowing it probably never would.

CHAPTER TWO

Kade zipped his duffel bag and gave the hotel room one last scan. Wallet, phone, keys—all accounted for. His redeye didn't leave until after midnight, which left him with too many hours to kill in Vegas with nothing to do but think. Dangerous territory.

Sully's wedding had been quick and perfect—twenty minutes at a chapel with fake flowers and real vows, followed by champagne toasts and his friend's ridiculous, love-struck grin. Now, down the hall, in a suite filled with more champagne and a field of chocolate-covered strawberries, the newlyweds were happily ensconced for the long weekend. Kade figured they probably wouldn't surface again any time soon, not even for food. Whoever said a man couldn't live on love alone had never met Sully and his bride—or, for that matter, any of the Sweet siblings.

Making his way down the elevator, he crossed the bustling lobby and checked out, leaving his duffel bag with the bell desk. Now, with nothing better to do, he wandered toward the casino floor, which beckoned him with its manufactured energy—the chiming of slots, the rattle of dice, the low murmur of voices. White noise for the brain. Perfect.

Kade found an empty spot at a blackjack table and slid into the chair, exchanging cash for chips. The dealer, a middle-aged man with efficient hands, nodded a greeting and drew the first cards from the dealer's shoe. Kade played mechanically, his mind only half on the cards. Hit. Stay. Double down. It was something to do with his hands while his thoughts wandered.

From his seat, he had a clear view of several other

tables. He was scanning the room, a habit ingrained by years of training, when a commotion from a nearby table pulled his attention. A man—forties, rumpled suit, clearly several drinks past his limit—was leaning heavily on the felt, his voice carrying over the ambient noise.

"Come on, sweetheart, smile for me," the drunk slurred at the dealer, a young woman with dark hair pulled back in a neat ponytail. "Pretty girl like you shouldn't look so serious."

From where he sat, he couldn't see her face, but he could see the tension in her shoulders. She dealt the next hand without acknowledging the comment.

The drunk lost a hand, and then another, his mood shifting from loud and annoying to louder and obnoxious. The sloppy man slapped the table. "Hit me again."

The dealer dealt him a card—nine of clubs. Bust.

His face reddened as she swept away his chips. "This is bullshit," he slurred. The guy was losing, and he was taking it out on her.

To her credit, the woman maintained her professional calm. This probably wasn't the first or last drunk she'd have to handle.

His own game forgotten, Kade watched the drunk grow louder and the dealer's stance stiffen. Where the hell was security?

The jerk lost another hand, the dealer reached to collect the chips, and the drunk's hand shot out and grabbed her wrist.

That was it. Kade's internal debate ended. He pushed his chair back, the legs scraping against the floor. He grabbed his chips and walked with a quiet, deliberate pace toward the other table. He didn't approach the drunk from the front. He came from behind, a silent shadow, and placed a hand, firm and heavy, on the man's shoulder. Controlling his own anger, using the sharp, clean edge of command, he stared the man down. "Let the lady go."

The man's hand fell away from the dealer's wrist as if he'd been burned. He spun around in his chair, his face a mask of belligerent rage, ready to fight. He found Kade standing perfectly still, his feet shoulder width apart, his hands clasped behind his back. Parade rest. It was an automatic, ingrained posture, a silent declaration of discipline and readiness that most civilians wouldn't recognize, but every bully understood.

The drunk's anger faltered. His gaze traveled from Kade's military-short haircut down to his well-shined leather shoes. The aggression in his eyes flickered, replaced by a glimmer of uncertainty. "Look, Mister..." he stammered.

Kade didn't move. Didn't blink. Didn't look away. "That's Sergeant First Class to you."

The man swallowed hard. He looked Kade over one more time, then his gaze slid to the dealer. "Fine. Let the b**ch steal your money." Scrambling to his feet, he gathered his chips and made a hasty, stumbling retreat into the casino crowd.

With the threat neutralized, Kade's posture relaxed. He turned his attention to the now-empty chair at the table. For the first time, he let himself really look at the dealer. Her professional mask was still in place, but he could see the relief in her eyes. They were green—a startling, vivid green that seemed out of place in the artificial light of the casino. She gave him a small, almost imperceptible nod, a silent acknowledgment of what had just happened.

He felt an unexpected pull, a desire to bridge the few feet of space between them. He walked to the empty chair and sat down, sliding his chips from the previous table onto the worn green felt. He looked directly at her, the rest of the casino fading into a muted, unimportant buzz. "Deal me in."

The felt under Cassidy's fingertips was a familiar, grounding texture in a world that had just been knocked slightly off-kilter. Her heart, which had been hammering a frantic, angry rhythm against her ribs, was slowly returning to its normal, steady beat, but adrenaline still hummed beneath her skin like a live wire. The drunk's grip on her wrist had been brief, but the memory of it lingered, making her hyperaware of every movement, every breath.

The drunk was gone. In his place sat a man who was the polar opposite: a quiet, solid presence whose stillness seemed to absorb the frantic energy of the casino. She dealt him his cards with practiced efficiency, but her attention kept snagging on details. The way he held his cards loosely, almost carelessly. The calm set of his shoulders. The fact that he wasn't looking at his hand at all—he was looking at her.

They played through several hands in a silence that should have been awkward but somehow wasn't. He hit on fourteen, busted, and didn't curse or complain. Just slid more chips forward for the next hand. The contrast to her usual clientele was stark. Most players at her table were running calculations, chasing systems, radiating desperation or bravado. This man was just… present. Grounded.

Another honeymoon couple on her left were oblivious, lost in their own world. The salesman on her right was too focused on his dwindling pile of chips to notice anything. But the man in what had been the drunk's chair—the Sergeant First Class—played with a calm, focused intensity. He wasn't a tourist looking for a thrill or a professional trying to beat the house. He played with a kind of disciplined logic, he played like a man who understood risk, but wasn't defined by it.

The minutes ticked by, each hand a small, contained world of its own. The charged silence between them was a strange kind of conversation. It felt safer, more real than any of the meaningless chatter she usually had to endure at her table.

The pit boss materialized at her elbow, tapping his watch. Shift change. Relief and disappointment hit simultaneously—relief at escaping the table, disappointment that she'd have to leave before she could properly thank the quiet stranger who'd stepped in when no one else had. She finished the hand, collected the cards, and began the familiar ritual of clearing her station. Taking a quick glance in his direction, she saw him cashing in his chips. Instead of disappearing into the casino crowd like every other player, he waited at the edge of the gaming area, his posture relaxed but attentive.

Cassidy's pulse kicked up for an entirely different reason than the drunk's harassment. She made her way toward the employee corridor, debating if she dared say something to the man. When he fell into step beside her, the decision was made. "I really appreciate the way you stepped in. He was definitely about to lose it."

"I noticed." A muscle along his jawline twitched with irritation before giving way to a soft smile. "Glad I was here to help."

"Unfortunately, these types of things happen more often than any of us like. Liquor and a losing streak is never a good combination."

"Agreed." The muscle in his jaw began to twitch again. "But there's something I don't understand."

Her steps slowed and she glanced up at him.

"Why didn't security step in?" There was an edge there, controlled but present. He'd been angry on her behalf. When was the last time anyone had been angry on her behalf?

Bobbing her head, she continued toward the employee area, wishing it were a farther away so she could talk a little longer. "They would have eventually. Some nights, they're spread a little thin. Tonight we had at least one or two call in sick."

"I see."

Only a few more feet of lobby and she'd be crossing into employee only territory. "Are you in town for long?"

He shook his head. "Just came in for a wedding last night to be best man for a buddy. Now I'm killing time until I go home on the redeye."

Home. The word hung in the air between them, a concept as foreign to Cassidy as a quiet night's sleep. He had a home to go to, a life that existed outside these walls. The thought sparked an impulse, a sudden, uncharacteristic urge to break her own routine. "Have you been to Vegas before?"

"No, ma'am."

Now that was a first. Ma'am. The man oozed chivalry and respect. "In that case, please let me give you a proper thank you. Show you a bit of the real Las Vegas before your flight."

At those words, his stomach rumbled loudly.

She couldn't help but smile; the brave knight in shining armor was hungry. "I'll feed you too."

"No, thank you." Again he shook his head. "You don't have to."

"I want to." Not till this very second did she realize just how much she wanted to. "Please."

He looked surprised, his eyebrows raising slightly. She felt a flush of heat creep up her neck. Way to make a fool of herself. Her lips moved, but she couldn't think of a graceful way to backpedal from her presumptive invitation.

All set to tell him not to worry, that she should go home and get some shut eye anyhow, the serious, focused expression on his face softened. A slow, genuine smile spread across his lips, reaching his eyes and making them sparkle with a warmth that was entirely unexpected. It transformed him, chasing away the shadows of the soldier and revealing the man underneath. "I think I'd like that." His voice came out low, a warm rumble that sent a shiver down her spine.

"Good." She tried not to squeal like a schoolgirl invited to the prom by the captain of the football team. "Give me ten minutes to change, then I'll show you the real Friday Night Vegas."

His grin widened. "Looking forward to it."

And much to her surprise, so the heck was she.

CHAPTER THREE

The automatic doors of the casino slid shut behind them, and the desert heat, dry and honest, settled over Kade. The cacophony of the casino floor faded, replaced by the distant hum of city traffic. Standing beside the woman who was about to show him the real Las Vegas, it struck him that he didn't even know her name. "I guess I should introduce myself properly. I'm Kade Sweet."

"Sweet?" A soft smile teased at her lips as she extended her hand. "It suits you. I'm Cassidy Barker."

"Nice to officially meet you." All his siblings had been razzed at one time or other over their last name, and there certainly was no shortage of teasing from the men he served with, at least at first, but she was the first to suggest the name suited him. "And thank you—I think."

"It was a compliment, I promise." She beamed at him.

Many a time he'd heard the word infectious in relation to another person's smile. Sort of like when one person in a theater laughs raucously, within moments, the whole place is doubled over in laughter. Her smile seemed to have the same power. There was no resisting the impulse to smile back. "Where to?"

"We need to get some food into that tummy of yours."

As if cued, his stomach rumbled again—loudly. "Good idea. I skipped breakfast and guess I skipped lunch too."

"Follow me, soldier."

She led him away from the main boulevard's overwhelming glare, turning down a side street where the buildings had character and the noise of the Strip faded. Tucked into a Chinatown strip mall, they settled at a small taqueria where the neon sign flashed and the smell of charred meat and fresh tortillas promised to satisfy anyone's appetite. Not what he'd expected to find in Chinatown, but then again, if he'd learned one thing in the military, it was never to be surprised.

"Tacos El Gordo." She slid into the vinyl booth across from him. "Best kept secret in Vegas. Well, not so secret anymore, but the tourists don't usually venture this far off the Strip."

"You come here often?" He tried to keep his tone casual, but found himself genuinely curious about the many sides of this particular woman.

"When I need to remember there's actual life beyond the casino floor." She unwrapped her first taco. "The adobada is the best. Try it."

He did. The spiced pork hit his tongue with a burst of flavor that made everything he'd eaten at the casino taste like cardboard in comparison. "Wow."

"Right?" Her smile was triumphant. "Told you."

After silently shoveling down a few mouthfuls, he glanced up at her. "How long have you lived in Las Vegas?"

"All my life." She shrugged. "Well, not in the city itself but the suburbs. I guess sort of all over."

"Sort of?" Something about the way she suddenly began picking at her food didn't sit right with him.

That shoulder hefted in another lazy shrug. "Foster kid. Moved around more than most."

His heart actually squeezed at the words. Having grown up in the same house as generations before him, he couldn't imagine being passed around from family to family like a hand-me-down pair of jeans. "Do you have any siblings?"

She shook her head in silence, still toying with the food on her plate.

No siblings. One more thing he couldn't imagine living without. No Garret, Preston, Carson, Jillian or Rachel. No one. All alone. A change of subject was in order before he wallowed in nostalgia. "How'd you wind up dealing in a casino?"

"Actually, it was the son of my last foster family. He's a

dealer here and thought that my ability to remember numbers made me a good candidate. He got me the job. How did you wind up in the…" her words hung.

"Army." He chuckled. "And honestly, I don't know. All my other siblings went to college. That had always been my plan. Then I ran into a K9 handler for the army and the next thing I knew, I was signing up. Been working with the best dogs on the planet ever since."

Her smile brightened. "I bet it's amazing working with dogs all day."

He couldn't help but smile back. "Ringo is my best friend. I can't imagine not working with K9s. It was hard leaving him with another handler while I'm going to be on temporary duty here in the States this coming year."

"That must be hard." She sighed. "I always wanted a dog, but not a great idea in an apartment."

"You'd like a house?"

She nodded. "Doesn't everyone?"

"Not always. Some people aren't meant for a cozy cottage with a white picket fence, a dog, and two point five children."

"And you would be one of those people?" Her question was honest.

Opening his mouth, all set to answer, he suddenly realized, he didn't have an honest answer. Only a few weeks ago he would have said yes without skipping a beat. Now, after spending a few days with his siblings and watching Sully take the final leap, well, now he wasn't so sure. "Maybe, maybe not."

"Sounds a little evasive. Care to share?"

Did he? Normally, he would divert the conversation to less personal matters, but instead, he found Cassidy easy to talk to and the words simply tumbled out. His dad's unexpected death, his siblings, the ranch, the thieving foreman, and how they stood to lose everything that had been in the Sweet family for generations.

"So, all your brothers and sisters agreed to marry for trust money?"

He bobbed his head, not quite believing that he'd

blabbed about everything from being swindled to his siblings falling one by one for their arranged spouses, to how confused everything had left him feeling. And maybe even a little guilty. "I thought they were nuts when they finally told me, but based on the circumstances, the idea had some merit. I actually felt a little guilty for a while that they had to risk so much while I was off safe from the scheme."

"Not so sure I'd say you were that safe. I don't know much about the military but I know that side of the world holds more risk than any arranged marriage might."

As much as he'd have loved to argue with her, the woman had a point. The last few years he'd been in a handful of very sketchy situations and was for the most part damn lucky that he and his team were still alive.

Turning Kade's words over in her head, Cassidy couldn't imagine what it must feel like to have siblings you love, land that has been in your family for years, never mind generations, and then to have someone come along and try to steal it all from you. Her heart actually ached for him. Especially the pain that lingered in his eyes. "It's not your fault."

His head snapped around to face her.

"You said you felt guilty being so far away and letting your siblings carry the burden of finding spouses to save the ranch. What you do is just as important as what they did."

He stared at her long and hard, his head tipping slightly to one side. "Thank you."

"For what?"

"For listening. For understanding." He shrugged. "Just thank you."

"Well," she pushed her chair back and stood, a new resolve settling over her, "come on. There's a lot to see and not a lot of time."

A slow, grateful smile spread across his face. "And where are we going now, tour guide?"

"To the heart of old Vegas." She led him out of the taqueria and back into the warm, buzzing night. "Fremont Street."

The moment they stepped onto the neon light-covered street, the energy shifted.

"Whoa." Kade stopped mid-step, tilting his head back to take it all in.

This was the Vegas of old that most people expected when they hit the strip. Bright neon lights and signs. Street performers—a man painted entirely in silver pretending to be a statue, a woman with a python wrapped around her shoulders—vied for attention.

Kade grinned, reminding her of a little kid the first time he met Mickey Mouse at Disneyland. "This is… a lot."

"And there's more." She tipped her head encouraging him to follow. Moving along, she pointed out the landmarks of her city—the Golden Nugget, Binion's, the El Cortez. They stopped to watch a surprisingly skilled magician make a tourist's watch disappear.

"Look," she pointed to a man in a white jumpsuit, his hair a perfect black pompadour, "an Elvis."

Kade chuckled. "I guess it wouldn't be Vegas without one."

"One?" She pointed in the opposite direction. "There's another one." A second, slightly less convincing Elvis serenaded a group of giggling women. "Little did the real Elvis know, after he died there'd be an Elvis on every corner in Las Vegas."

Kade shook his head, a genuine, easy laugh rumbling in his chest. It was a good sound, a sound that for just a moment made her wish he didn't have a plane to catch in a few hours. They continued walking, taking in all the sights and sounds that were strictly Vegas.

Kade studied a weathered neon sign carefully. "This is quite the show, but I can't fathom living here twenty-four seven. Sort of like Disney World; a nice place to visit but living there all the time would be a bit like Alice having fallen down the rabbit hole."

That made her chuckle, she'd never thought to compare

Vegas to Disney or Alice in Wonderland, and yet, he'd nailed it. Suddenly, as if to prove his point, the LED canopy above them exploded into a full light show—thousands of feet of synchronized imagery and sound transformed the street. All around them tourists and locals began to dance where they stood, whether on the sidewalk or in the middle of the street. Some quite good, others, well, two left feet came to mind.

A moment taking it all in and one of the multi-footed dancers bumped into Cassidy, sending her full force into Kade. Pressed against him, her hands splayed across his chest, she blinked at the unexpected energy sizzling under her fingertips.

Slowly, the startled look in Kade's eyes shifted to sheer amusement. His lips tipped up at the corners, and that amused glint turned mischievous. "When in Rome, do like the Romans. Shall we?"

Taking hold of her hand, his fingers circled around hers and then with the slightest flick of his wrist, he had her spinning out and then curled her back in again. The unexpected dance move had her head tipping back and a bubble of laughter escaping. Her other hand on her chest, she actually giggled as he had her bopping back and forth and spinning like one of the awkward celebrity contestants on *Dancing With the Stars* made to look good by their professional partner. Another burst of laughter erupted and she had to ask herself: when was the last time she'd had this much fun?

The tempo slowed along with the light show above and on a regretful sigh, she tugged him down the street toward a doorway from which the sound of a raucous, sing-along piano spilled out. "This is a Vegas highlight for any true music lover."

The piano bar was packed, the energy infectious. They had to stand in line for a few minutes before a couple people left and they were allowed in. Dark paneling surrounded the room, dim lights kept the patrons incognito, only the two back-to-back grand pianos were illuminated under bright spotlights.

Easily the one player shifted from Three Dog Night's song "Jeremiah Was a Bullfrog" to the Brazilian hit "Girl from Ipanema." To her surprise, it seemed as if everyone in the place, regardless of their years, knew the lyrics. Even Kade, who she'd thought would be more reserved, was singing loudly now to Michael Bublé's "Haven't Met You Yet."

The waitress came over, handed them a menu with a short list of bar food and a longer list of drinks. Perusing the options Kade glanced at his watch. "Still have a couple of hours, I guess it will be safe to try their famous Punchbowl." Putting the menu down, he bobbed his head at the next tune to play and leaned into her. "Quite the music variety," he said, his fingers tapping to the beat. "No wonder you like this place."

"I've actually never been here before."

His eyes rounded in surprise. "You're kidding?"

"Nope." She shook her head. "Though it's quite famous. Everyone is always talking about it, I just never gotten around to coming." She wasn't going to say she didn't have any close friends and it seemed rather pathetic to come alone. She was glad to finally have an excuse to check it out in person, and was a little sorry she hadn't done so sooner. This was proving to be more fun than she'd expected. "I do hear that the reason that signature drink is called the Punchbowl is because it packs quite a punch."

"Now I *have* to try it."

The waitress came back and Kade ordered a mixed cheeseboard and two Punchbowls. When the drinks arrived, the sheer size of the tall curvy shaped glass gave her pause. The thing was probably at least twenty-four ounces of punch. She was definitely going to take this one very slow.

Kade lifted his drink, and she did the same. Glasses clinking against the next ivory pounding tune, his voice carried over the song, "To pleasant surprises. Cheers."

"Cheers," she echoed, wishing they had more than a few hours left.

CHAPTER FOUR

An ice pick seemed to be stabbing at Kade's temple. Sucking in a deep breath, he made a valiant effort to pry one eye open. The morning light beaming through the crack in the curtains had him slamming his eyes shut again. Not the best idea he'd ever had.

Rubbing his eyes, he shook his head in a vain effort to clear his mind. Regret for moving his aching head shot through him as sharply as the prick of that ice pick. Where the heck was he?

Once again lifting his lids, slowly, he took in the wall in front of him, a massive flamingo painting on one side of the curtains. Beside that a standard issue corner chair and lamp. A hotel. He was definitely in a hotel. The bright light shining into the room meant—morning. *His flight.* Crap. He must have missed his flight. Wiping at his forehead with both hands, a muffled moan startled him. Turning toward the sound, his gaze landed on the lump beside him. *Aw, hell.* He wasn't alone.

Two slender, firm arms stretched out from beneath the sheets. Blinking, he focused on the swath of dark hair fanned across the pillow. Another moment and the lump shifted, giving him a birds eye view of a beautiful sleeping face. Cassidy. *Blast.* He didn't need X-ray vision to know that she wasn't wearing much, if anything, under that sheet. Scraping his hands down his face, he heaved a deep sigh. What had he done? She was a nice girl. Most definitely younger than him. According to his calculations, by almost a decade. He hadn't known her long, but any fool could see she wasn't the sort for waking up in hotel rooms with near strangers. Damn it. Now what?

Sitting up, he spun around, setting his feet on the ground, his gaze falling on the nightstand. Or more so, a sheet of beige paper with ornate blue scrolling, large print and a golden stamp. Blinking to focus, he stretched out one hand, closed his fingers on the corner and bringing it closer, carefully read: Cassidy Anne Barker. Kade Eric Sweet. No one but Uncle Sam used his middle name. His gaze shifted to the key words underneath their names. Like a bolt of lightning, a shock ripped through him. In large, bold, black letters the words Marriage License might as well have been in pink neon. *Holy hell.* At least now he knew what he'd done. Oh, lord.

Some serious conversation needed to happen and he wasn't going to do it sitting in bed stark naked. Or without caffeine. The ache in his head and fog in his brain would require lots of caffeine. Easing off the bed, he inched slowly toward the bathroom door in search of... where were his pants? The bathroom was empty. Still in the doorway, he turned to scan the bedroom, his gaze drifted to the other side of the bed. Her side.

Like bread crumbs to the witch's cottage, a line of clothing—pants, shirts, boxers, panties, a bra—made a trail from the front door to the bed. Good heavens. Unless they'd both passed out upon collapsing on that massive bed, logic told him any chance of an annulment had flown out the window long before sunrise.

Quietly crossing the carpet, he grabbed what was his in one arm, and picking up her things, he set them on the chair in the corner. Taking a moment to look at Cassidy—she seemed so peaceful, so content, like a sweet angel—his chest constricted. How the heck was he going to fix this?

Shaking his head, he used the pain to snap his attention away from the woman that he had no business staring at, legal wife or not, and returned to the bathroom. Door closed behind him, he finger-brushed his teeth, splashed water on his face, and donned his clothing as quickly as possible.

Now all he had to do was remember what the heck happened. How had they gone from a drink at a fun piano bar to a marriage license in a Vegas hotel room? He had very vivid and clear memories of dancing in the street, singing along with the piano players, laughing, ordering another one of those addictive fruit flavored beverages. Or was it two more?

Raking his fingers through his hair, his gaze fell once again on Cassidy. This was so not like him. He never gets memory-erasing drunk, and he doesn't do one night stands, not even when his buddies were out and about de-stressing with the local ladies. He liked to know his companions for more than a few hours. Like the tip of your tongue repeatedly drawn to the empty spot where a tooth had been lost, his gaze kept returning to that piece of paper. Married. Apparently, he still didn't do one night stands.

A prickly feeling at the back of her neck drew Cassidy from the nicest dream. Not that she had any idea what she'd dreamed, but she felt so good, it had to have been wonderful. So why did she have an uneasy feeling, like she was being watched, which was ridiculous since she lived alone.

Ignoring the unease, and enjoying that unexpected morning feeling of utter contentment, she stretched her arms and opened her eyes. Thankful for the day off and not needing to hurry, she frowned at the ceiling. Where were the stains from last year's roof leak? Squeezing her eyes shut then open again, she stared harder. That was not her ceiling. Springing up to a seated position, her eyes almost bugged out of her head. Across from her, in an upholstered chair, his hands folded and resting on his knees, Kade sat watching her.

Instinctively, she grabbed the edge of the sheet, pulling it up in front of her to cover her nightgown—that she wasn't wearing. *Holy hell.* What had she done?

"It's not what you think." His expression was flat, unemotional, and unreadable.

Her gaze drifted down to the sheet pulled up to her chin,

around the room, then back to him. "I don't see how it can be anything other than what this looks like."

His head tipped to one side. She turned to follow his gaze, her own landing on a sheet of paper on her nightstand. Shifting her grip on the sheet to her right hand, her left stretched out to retrieve the page. Her jaw dropped and her head snapped up to face him.

"You don't remember either?"

Immediately, her gaze fell to the page. Marriage License. "I'm going to say no."

"Your clothes are on the chair over there." Kade pointed to the corner of the room, pushed to his feet, and strode to the window, his back to the bed—and her. "If you'd like to get dressed."

If the entire scenario weren't so…unsettling, she would have laughed. The evidence at hand indicated that he'd already seen pretty much all of her, yet chivalry had him turning away to allow her to dress. Or was it remorse? Either way, despite whatever this was, she really did like this man.

Still clutching the sheet to her front, she stood, dragging the sheet off the bed and kicking it around her like a Grecian robe. Hurrying to the chair, she snatched up her clothing and shuffled to the bathroom. Door closed behind her, she stared at her reflection in the mirror. Her mind struggled to put together the pieces of last night. Splashing water on her face, she washed up quickly even if she had to wear yesterday's clothes, and wondered how could she possibly not remember getting married? She wasn't a drinker, that was no secret, and she might have gotten giddy a time or two, but she'd also never drawn a complete blank on what she'd done the night before.

"Married," she muttered to the empty room.

Fully dressed, she faced the closed door, sucked in a deep fortifying breath. Hands a little shaky, she turned the knob, swinging the door open.

The sound of the door had Kade turning around to face her, the slightest of smiles teased at the corner of his mouth. She really wanted to smile back, but somehow, fear had her barely able to remain standing. What was a person supposed to do when they woke up married to a stranger?

"You look lovely."

Now she laughed. "Are you always this charming?"

Thankfully, he chuckled too. "It helps when it's the truth."

Heat instantly flooded her cheek.

His smile widened. "And even lovelier when you blush." Crossing the room to one of the two vacant chairs, he took a seat. "I ordered us breakfast. Didn't know if you liked coffee or tea, or both, or cereal or eggs, so I ordered it all."

She felt one brow rise high on her forehead. He may not know it, but yes, the man was always charming. "That was thoughtful. A hot cup of tea would be really nice about now." Though the thought of eating actual food made her stomach turn, she suspected that nourishment was at least one of the things she needed. An escape route might not be a bad thing either. Following his lead, she walked to the other chair and sat down.

Silence hung for several long seconds that felt more like hours.

"What do you remember?" he finally asked.

Her cheeks tugged at her lips as her mind played back most of yesterday. "I remember you rescuing me from an obnoxious drunk. I remember eating at the taqueria." Her smile widened. "I remember dancing in the street. By the way, you are a really good dancer."

"Thank you. So are you."

"That's news to me."

"You followed my lead easily. I actually thought you might have had dance lessons or something."

She shook her head. "That was the first time I'd ever done more than sway on a dance floor." She threaded her hands together and tried not to fidget. "I remember going to the piano bar, ordering a Punchbowl, singing 'Sweet Caroline' over and over."

"So far, I'm with you." He leaned back in the chair. "I think I remember ordering a second Punchbowl."

"Actually," she stared at the ceiling, "I think you ordered two more. I vaguely remember thinking what a great ability to hold your liquor you had."

"Hmm," he practically scoffed.

"Now things get fuzzy. I know we were worried you'd miss your flight, so we left." She squinted as if that would help clear the fog in her brain. "Elvis! I remember there was an Elvis outside."

Kade squinted at the ceiling. "That's right. He was handing out flyers."

"Everyone in Vegas hands out flyers pimping one business or other." She continued flipping the memories in her head. "I'm drawing a blank—no, wait." She held up a finger. "The flyer was for one of those specialty, quick and easy wedding chapels."

"Like ordering a square burger at White Castle?" The question was clear in his tone.

She nodded. "Yeah."

"We went inside." It wasn't really a question, but she nodded again. "Everyone was dressed like Elvis."

Pictures were coming up in her mind. "We joked there must be an Elvis convention in town."

Bobbing his head, he chuckled. "That's right. I said how could a wedding in a place like that be legal, and you told me a wedding in Vegas is a legally binding wedding no matter who the preacher was."

"I doubt Elvis was a preacher." She looked at the license again, curious who signed it. "Albert Gleeson JCC. Justice of the City Courts."

"And Elvis impersonator," Kade muttered.

Room service arrived with food and beverage. Kade directed him to put the tray on the table. He gave the man a cash tip and proceeded to pour her a cup of tea. "Cream or sugar?"

"Milk, no sugar." She accepted the cup he handed her and waited for him to pour his own coffee. This man was racking up the good guy points. Thoughtful, considerate, calm. Any of the men she'd known in her life, however briefly, would have been blowing steam out of their ears by now. Picking up a piece of toast, she took a sip of her tea, watching Kade inhale his coffee and devour a breakfast sandwich. When they'd each finished their first cups and gone for refills, she sat down again and finally spoke. "What I can't remember or figure out, is why did we get married?"

Downing the last sip of his second cup, Kade set the empty mug down on the nightstand. "Your lease is up."

"What?"

"The cobwebs are clearing out. You told me that your lease is up, the rent is going up, and there are no cheaper decent apartments available. I mentioned you should move to Texas."

"That's right." Her cobwebs, as he put it, were clearing too. "Wide-open spaces, beautiful sunsets, and lots of good colleges."

"You talked about going back to school. Doing something different with your life."

She nodded. All of it was true, but sadly, talk was probably all it would ever be.

Pinching the bridge of his nose, he heaved a deep sigh. "And that's when I suggested if you come home with me and play Mrs. Kade Sweet, after the first year and the big payout, I would give you enough for a down payment on a house of your own."

Suddenly the entire conversation replayed in her mind. "I said yes."

"And we got married." His gaze darted to the bed and back. "I would've been gone most of the time anyhow whether TDY or returning to my team. I promised in name only. No hanky-panky. No shenanigans." He snuck another sideways glance at the bed. "I'm sorry. Note to self: stop after one Punchbowl."

"Ditto." Shifting in her seat, she tried to understand all the emotions running through her. Confusion, embarrassment, a little fear, and a lot of regret. But the surprising thing was the regret. Not for what she'd done, but that she wouldn't get a chance to accompany this man to Texas and help save his ranch.

His "I don't suppose…" tumbled over her "What if…"

They both laughed. That was something else they'd done a lot last night. Both before and after the impromptu Elvis wedding.

"You first," he offered.

"Okay." She struggled for the right words. "Maybe, even though we were definitely three sheets to the wind, maybe the plan isn't so crazy."

His eyes widened.

"I mean, you do need a wife and I need a change."

"You'd do that?"

How could she explain she'd never had anything really her own, no purpose, and frankly, no place had ever felt like home. What did she have to lose testing the waters in Texas? "If you'd like me to."

"Just to clarify, you're proposing we follow through with the original drunken agreement? A pretend marriage to fool my mom and the bank and secure the ranch?"

Afraid to say the wrong thing, she merely nodded.

A smile slowly took over his face. "Well, Mrs. Sweet. It looks like I'm going to have to book another seat back home." His brows suddenly buckled and he looked at her through a frown.

"Change your mind already?" She made it sound like a tease, but she was praying he hadn't.

"No." He shook his head. "It just struck me, how am I going to explain to my mother that I was married by an Elvis impersonator?"

CHAPTER FIVE

Standing inside Cassidy's apartment, Kade understood a little better why leaving wasn't difficult for her. The furnishings were neat and clean, but sparse. The kitchen and bathroom appeared to be near original, which made them older than him.

"It will only take me a few to pack," she called from the bedroom.

He walked over to the doorway. "Can I help?"

Standing in front of her closet, staring at the clothes hanging from the rod, she sighed. "Is it cold in Texas?"

"In the winter, yes."

Her head bobbed as she fingered a few sundresses.

"It's also pretty darn hot in the summer." His gaze drifted to the two suitcases resting on her bed. It dawned on him that she expected to pack her entire world in two suitcases. He should probably offer to store her belongings for the year. "I could look into storage units for whatever you're not taking with you."

Grabbing an armful of clothes, she spun about. "There's nothing here I want to keep. I've already texted a friend from work. She's going to come by, get my key, take what she wants, and sell the rest."

"Are you sure?"

Her gaze scanned the room that reminded him more of an efficient bachelor pad than the warm and welcoming home you'd expect from a woman. "I'm sure."

By the time she'd filled the two suitcases with her clothing and a small toiletry bag, her friend had arrived, gleeful to have a free shopping spree and promising to send Cassidy fifty percent of whatever she earned from the sales.

A pang of guilt stabbed at him. How could he possibly ask anyone to leave their world behind to play house with him for one year? Had he ever done anything more selfish in his life? It wasn't like this was life or death, or that the ranch was in the same dire straits as several months ago.

While the friend was opening and closing kitchen cabinets he walked up to Cassidy, standing over a dresser.

"It's all second hand."

"Excuse me?"

She closed the lid on a small wooden box and tucked it into the still open suitcase. "Everything in here is second-hand. Most of it I picked from the trash. Didn't even pay for it."

That surprised him. Not that it was second-hand, but nothing looked as though it had been scavenged from a dumpster.

"So you can relax."

Now his eyes popped.

A smile replaced the lost look he'd seen in her eyes a moment ago. "Did you know you're easy to read?"

Was he? He shook his head.

"Maybe not to everyone on the street. But kids in foster care learn how to read the lightest of nuances. We have to know if we're wading into dangerous waters, or able to bask in the sunshine."

"Interesting metaphors." And he didn't like the idea that she'd had to learn to read people to protect herself. That, of course, wasn't exactly what she'd said, but it was clear nonetheless, and he didn't like it. Not one bit.

"I just want you to know that leaving all this behind seems to be harder on you than me."

Heaving a sigh, he studied her. "You're sure?"

"Are you going to spend the next year asking me that?" Her smile softened her words.

He bit back a smile. "I'll try not to."

"Good." She closed the suitcase, zipped it shut, and looking around the room nodded. "Ready when you are."

Once again, he was booked on the red-eye to Midland with a stopover in Dallas. Only this time he was traveling with a wife. Sort of. They said little on the cab ride to the airport. He kept an eye on her as they drove through the city, looking for any signs of regret, or simply changing her mind. Priding himself on also being able to read people, he saw nothing. Her expression was as blank as a new sheet of paper.

Not wanting to surprise too many people, once they'd checked in, he excused himself and walked to a quiet corner and called Preston. He'd texted already that he'd missed his flight and would be home tomorrow morning, but hadn't said anything else.

"Hey, bro. You planning on missing the flight again?" His brother wasn't nearly as funny as he gave himself credit for.

"Ha ha. Listen. There's been a little change of plan." Little—was that ever an understatement.

"Oh?" His single word response held more hesitancy than surprise.

"I sort of got married."

"Sort of?" This time shock clearly tinged Preston's voice.

"Okay. I got married."

"I thought we told you we didn't need that much more money."

"You did. And that's not why I got married."

"Oh?" This time his voice straddled somewhere between surprise and doubt.

"But it is why we're staying married."

"Oh."

"Can't you say anything else?"

"Sure. What the hell are you talking about?"

As quickly as he could he explained about meeting Cassidy, going out on the town, having more fun than he'd had in a very long time, and waking up married.

"And she understands that Mom doesn't know about the marriage scheme?"

He nodded, his gaze on her sitting quietly across the gate area, watching him watch her. "She does. I think it will be fine. A good thing. I mean, we can use the extra money, right?"

"You know we can." Preston went quiet for a long minute. "I'll give the others a heads up. What do you want me to say to Mom?"

"Nothing. This isn't something I want to spring on her over the phone."

"I'm not so sure that springing it on her in person is going to be any better."

"I know, but that's what I'm going with."

"Understood. I'll see you both tomorrow."

"Okay."

"And Kade?"

"Yes?"

"Congratulations, big brother."

Miles and miles of open land stretched in every direction, broken only by fence lines that seemed to go on forever and clusters of cattle grazing in the distance. Somehow the sky felt bigger here, bluer, not a single cloud to be seen for miles. The drive from the Midland airport had been long, flat, and uneventful. As Kade turned off the main road onto a long, gravel driveway, his truck kicked up a puff of the dusty Texas dirt that had surrounded them most of the morning. Her first glimpse of the Sweet Ranch unfolding before her, Cassidy peered through the windshield.

In the distance, a massive house, a sprawling fortress of stone and timber, stood against the vast, open sky. It was exactly as Kade had described it, yet seeing it in person felt different, more real. More intimidating. Barns and outbuildings dotted the landscape, and the sheer scale of the place was staggering. This wasn't just a home; it was a legacy.

Her fingers gripped the edge of the dashboard, not from fear, but from the sudden overwhelming sense that she'd stepped into a different universe. One where people owned land measured in acres instead of square feet. Where families stayed for generations instead of foster placements measured in months.

"You okay?" Kade glanced over at her, concern creasing the edges of his eyes.

She nodded slowly. "It's... big." The word felt ridiculously inadequate.

"It's home."

Home. The word rattled around in her chest, foreign and familiar all at once. She'd never had a home. Not a real one. Only once had she come close, but even that had in the end proven to be temporary. Everything in her life had been temporary.

The car came to a stop in front of the house and a woman emerged onto the sprawling front porch, wiping her hands on an apron. She was smaller than Cassidy had imagined, but she moved with a quiet, undeniable strength. This had to be Alice Sweet.

"Ready?" Kade asked quietly.

Was she? Cassidy sucked in a breath and reached for the door handle. "As I'll ever be."

Kade was out of the car before Cassidy could unbuckle her seatbelt. His hand extended to her, she exited the old truck and he shortened his long strides to match hers. Unsteady legs moved one in front of the other. This was it. The point of no return.

"Thought you were going to be home yesterday." Alice gave her son a soft smile and gentle kiss on the cheek. The gesture made Cassidy smile, such genuine maternal affection. Then the woman's gaze shifted to Cassidy, her eyes, the same piercing blue as Kade's, filled with a gentle curiosity.

His hand found the small of her back in a gesture that was both a steadying presence and a silent claim. "Mom, this is Cassie."

Cassie? Where had that come from? She shot him a quick, questioning look, but he was focused entirely on his mother. Cassie—she kind of liked it. New name for the new her.

"It's a pleasure to meet you," Alice said, her smile not quite reaching her eyes. There was a reservation there, a mother's natural caution.

"The pleasure is all mine." Without any thought, Cassidy's hand gravitated toward Kade's like a magnet seeking true north, relieved to discover his hand reaching for her as well. Strong fingers wrapped around hers, channeling strength and support through that simple contact. She held on tight.

His mother's gaze followed the movement, her eyes studious, pensive, as if able to see past the façade and read every thought and memory.

Kade squeezed her hand, a silent signal. "She's my wife."

Dark eyebrows rose high over deep blue penetrating eyes and Cassidy's stomach lurched high in her throat, almost robbing her of any air.

Her gaze shifting from her son to Cassidy, a slow, radiant smile bloomed across Alice Sweet's face, transforming her features and making her eyes sparkle. "I see," then she stepped forward, her arms open, and pulled Cassidy into a fierce, welcoming hug.

Startled, Cassidy stood stiffly for a moment before releasing Kade's hand, drawing her own arms up and returning the warm welcome.

This was so much more than a business deal. She was standing on the porch of a home that had stood for generations, beside a man she barely knew but was legally bound to, being hugged by a mother-in-law who had just accepted her without a single question. This was a whole new kind of crazy.

When Alice finally pulled back, her eyes were bright. "Come on in, both of you. I've got a pot roast in the oven and you must be exhausted from all that traveling." She looked at Kade with that same knowing smile. "We'll get you both settled."

Cassidy glanced up at Kade as they crossed the threshold, their hands still linked. He met her gaze and gave her fingers a gentle squeeze.

She didn't understand how she could be welcomed so easily, no questions, no complaints, no rants, no insults.

This world she'd slipped into was proving more bizarre than she could ever have imagined. Walking inside with her hand once again firmly ensconced in Kade's, there was only one thing she was sure of: whatever came next, at least they were in this together.

CHAPTER SIX

The moment his mother's arms wrapped around Cassidy, every anxious nerve in his body relaxed. He hadn't realized how tense he'd been until that simple gesture of acceptance. His mom didn't ask questions, didn't demand explanations—she just welcomed. That was Alice Sweet in a nutshell. The front door hadn't even clicked shut behind them before Alice was herding them toward the kitchen, the scent of pot roast and something warm and cinnamon-spiced wrapping around Kade like the hug his mother had just bestowed on Cassidy. His mom was most definitely in her element, a whirlwind of happy energy as she pulled out glasses for tea. Her easy acceptance was the best-case scenario.

"May I help?" Cassidy eased away from Kade and moved toward his mother.

"Nonsense. For today, you're a guest. Tomorrow you can help."

Cassidy glanced at him, looking for what? Approval, advice? Not sure what she wanted, he nodded, smiled, and she immediately returned to his side. Apparently, silent communication between married people began early in a relationship regardless of how strong that relationship was. And wasn't that an interesting little discovery.

"I suppose we'll have to set you two up. You certainly can't spend your honeymoon in his old room."

"Mom," he practically groaned.

"What?" His mother stopped short and spun around to face Kade. "This is your honeymoon. I mean, how long have you been married—two days?"

And so the questions were about to begin. "We were

married day before yesterday," Kade volunteered before Cassidy could.

His mom bobbed her head, seemed to relax. "Yes, well, I'll talk to Jillian, see how long…"

"No need." Jillian came in the back door. "Blake and I are moving the last of our things over to the new house." Casually, she strolled over to her brother and gave him a quick peck on the cheek, then turned to face her new sister-in-law. "Welcome." Then so no one could see, she mouthed, "Thank you."

And now the true rapid fire of questions began. Placing two tall glasses of tea on the table, his mom gestured for everyone to take a seat. "So, how did you two meet?"

To her credit, Cassidy smiled sweetly. "Kade rescued me."

Alice froze mid motion.

"From a drunk."

Now his mom blinked, her gaze narrowed in confusion.

"I'm—I mean, I was a dealer at a casino. This one drunk was losing and getting rather…obnoxious. When he grabbed my hand, your son intervened." He had no idea if she was truly that grateful or one hell of an actress, but she turned to level her gaze with his that actually had Jillian sighing.

"Okay." His mother smiled. "My son played knight in shining armor."

Blushing, Cassie nodded. "Since he only had one day in town, and I was off shift, it seemed that the least I could do was show him around town."

More questions came at them as more siblings came through the door, each trying rather unsuccessfully to deflect their mother. By sticking to the truth, it was pretty easy to get through the inquisition, but Kade noticed Cassidy's smile becoming just a fraction tighter with each inquiry.

The corners of Alice Sweet's mouth curled into a huge grin. "So what you're telling me is that this was love at first sight."

"Really, Mom," Rachel interrupted while Kade and

Cassie once again glanced at each other, not wanting to lie, but needing to keep up the charade.

On a deep sigh, Alice's smile slipped. "At least tell me if it was a nice wedding?"

Pushing to his feet, he looked to his mother. "You know how much you love Elvis Presley music?"

His mom nodded.

"Well, then you would have loved the ceremony. Now, if it's okay with you, I thought I'd take Cassidy to the barn, show her what she's getting into."

His teasing tone had his mother grinning even wider. "Of course. Dinner won't be ready for a bit more. Take your time."

He led her out the back door, the screen door slapping shut behind them. Cassidy hesitated beside him, her gaze sweeping over the sprawling landscape, over the horses roaming in the paddock, the cows and their new offspring grazing in the distance. Sheer reverence and awe shone in her eyes.

"Ever seen a cow before?"

Her head shifted left then right. "Only in pictures. Same with horses."

"Hey," Preston called from just outside the barn, walking briskly to catch up to them. "Sorry. I really wanted to be back at the house before you got here to help run interference with Mom. But we had a mare reject her foal and I've been scrambling." He came to a stop in front of Cassidy. "Welcome to the family, and thank you."

Her one brow lifted but nodding slightly all she said was "thank *you*."

Preston turned to face him. "How did Mom take it?"

"Better than I thought. Though, I suspect the questions are going to get tougher before they get easier."

"Agreed. We'll help where we can. As we've done with the rest of us, you two will have the master. King bed makes the charade a little easier to handle." His gaze drifted to Cassidy and back to Kade. "That is unless true congratulations are in order?"

Resisting the urge to tackle his brother for putting her

on the spot like that, he took a deep breath before responding to his brother through tightly clamped teeth. "It's business. Temporary."

"Got it." Preston nodded. "I'd better go clean up for dinner. Hear what Mom has to say after greeting you two."

"Thanks." Kade hugged his brother. "For everything."

"You know us." He stepped out of the embrace. "One for all and…"

"All for one," Kade finished, took hold of Cassidy's hand and proceeded toward the barn. They walked a few feet before he spoke without looking at her. "Do you mind this?" He lifted their clasped hands.

"No," she responded without hesitation.

"We're going to have to play the part for Mom. Little things like this need to be natural."

"Of course."

Inside the barn, a few of the horses poked their heads over their stall doors, dark eyes gleaming with curiosity.

Her eyes wide, Cassidy moved slowly, cautiously, as if having entered the sacred halls of a grand cathedral. Her voice low and soft, she glanced up at him. "They're beautiful."

That was not what he'd expected, even though he agreed that horses were some of the most majestic animals on earth.

Pausing at the first stall, her hand slowly moved forward, palm up, letting the horse sniff her hand as if she were approaching a skittish canine. When the horse kissed her palm, she giggled. Not a lick of fear in her. That was a good thing, for the most part.

"This is Boots. She's one of the gentlest horses on the ranch." At least she used to be. A pang of something akin to regret or perhaps shame washed over him at the realization that he had no clue if the ranch had acquired gentler, sweeter animals. "Next time we'll bring some apples or carrots. I have a feeling you'll have them all eating out of your hand in no time, both literally and figuratively."

"I'd like that."

And he liked that she seemed to be taking so much in

stride. Though it hurt him to think that was probably a long-ago acquired skill learned from years of being passed around from family to family, never knowing what situation she might be tossed into.

In the distance he heard Carson calling from the house. "Table's set. We're all ready to gnaw on wood."

Cassidy frowned and Kade bit back a laugh. "I think that's our cue to face more music."

Her shoulders straightened and some of the light in her eyes gave way to a hint of nervous anticipation.

"It'll be fine. You're doing great."

"Thank you. I'm trying."

"And succeeding."

They'd barely set foot in the kitchen when his nephew Mason flew across the room and skidded to a halt in front of him and Cassidy. "Are you Uncle Kade's new wife?"

Cassidy blinked, then quickly gathered her composure and squatted to his height. "I am."

"I want a cousin. Are you going to have a baby?"

The room erupted. Alice gasped, half-horrified, half-amused. Jess swooped in to scoop up her son, her cheeks a bright, furious red. "Mason! We do not ask people questions like that!"

Carson was laughing so hard he had to lean against the wall for support.

Gathering his own composure, he leaned in to answer for her, when to his surprise, she smiled at the presumptive boy.

"Well," she said, her voice full of gentle gravity, "I guess we'll just have to see, won't we?"

The dining room was a master class in controlled chaos, a world away from the quiet, solitary meals Cassidy was used to. Standing in the doorway, she took in the sheer magnitude of the nightly event, the long expanse of polished wood, the mismatched chairs that somehow all fit together, the platters of food being set on the table. So many people. She'd practiced the names of the siblings and their spouses before leaving Vegas, on the plane, and on the drive to the ranch, yet she still wasn't sure she could remember who was who without fumbling at least a name or two—or three.

"Kade, take your regular place by Preston. Cassie, you sit to Kade's other side."

Nodding her head, she turned toward Kade. His hand found the small of her back, guiding her forward when her feet seemed reluctant to cooperate. He pulled out a chair for her, waited until she sat, then settled into the seat beside her. That small gesture made the overwhelming tableau slightly more manageable. Still a tad terrifying, but manageable. It helped knowing everyone at the table, except for Mrs. Sweet, knew the truth of their arrangement. What none of them knew, however, was how many nights she'd dreamed of a family just like this one. Loud, close, and there for each other.

Mrs. Sweet sat at the head of the table. "Pass the potatoes down, Carson. Garret, don't let that gravy bowl sit there getting cold."

Plates moved with practiced efficiency, hands reaching and passing without anyone needing to ask twice. Cassidy accepted each dish as it came to her. Pot roast, mashed potatoes, green beans with bacon, fresh rolls still steaming, butter in a glass dish. Why weren't these people as big as a house?

"So, Cassie," Alice's voice was gentle, and comforting, "have you always lived in Las Vegas?"

The table quieted slightly, everyone continuing to eat but clearly listening.

"Yes, ma'am." She swallowed hard. This was it. The moment of truth—or at least most of it. Just enough not to get tangled in a web of lies, but not enough to reveal the true nature of their arrangement. "I've lived all over Nevada. Foster care."

For just a moment, she saw a flicker of something akin to pain in Alice Sweet's eyes. Just as quickly, a curtain of pleasantry descended and Alice smiled. "Do you like it there?"

"It was okay, but I don't think the flash and bling could ever compete with what you have here."

"Oh, we have plenty of bling," Jillian teased.

Rachel chuckled beside her sister. "Our aunts own the Corn Hole Heaven shop. You see, Honeysuckle is the corn hole capital of Texas and bling seems to be growing in popularity. Just ask Mildred McEntire."

Cassidy blinked. "Corn hole?"

"The game," Kade prompted. When her expression didn't change, his gaze narrowed at her. "Have you never played corn hole?"

She shook her head.

"Oh boy," someone said and the next thing she knew they were all babbling over each, wrestling for who was going to introduce her to the game, what weight bags she had to have, and who would partner with her at the next local tournament.

Who knew an entire town, never mind state, could be so animated over what she now understood to be a backyard game, and according to most of the siblings, better than horseshoes or croquet combined.

By the time people started to stand and clear the table, Cassidy almost felt as if she'd always been a part of this raucous family. Kade's mother was being so kind and sweet and sensitive, Cassidy just knew the woman was dying to ask some serious questions about their meeting and whirlwind marriage, but she didn't. She tread carefully and made Cassidy feel so much at home that she already felt absolutely horrible about deceiving this nice lady. Even if it was supposedly for her own good.

She and Kade were relegated to the living room for dessert. She'd come within inches of taking a seat in the comfy looking upholstered chair when it struck her that newlyweds would want to sit close. She headed for the sofa, more pleased than she should have been when Kade sat beside her. Not too close to invade her personal space, but close enough for his mother to think they actually loved each other.

With everyone seated in the massive living room, every time Kade's mom seemed to be on the verge of asking more about the sudden wedding to a near stranger, one of the siblings distracted her. They were awfully sweet. It made her smile how much they loved their mother, their ranch, and yes, their brother too. She liked feeling caught up in the protective wave that covered Kade, and by association, her. That would be twice in as many days that someone had stepped forward to protect her. A girl could get used to that.

The next thing she learned was that in ranching country, where ranchers rose before the sun, they also went to bed early. One by one the siblings bid their goodnights to their mother and each other, Carson and his wife and son the only ones still living in the main house.

"Shall we?" Speaking softly, Kade extended his hand to her.

Taking hold of the proffered hand, they climbed the stairs in silence, Kade a half step ahead, leading the way. The master bedroom door was open, light spilling into the hallway. Kade closed the door quietly behind them, and suddenly the room felt much smaller.

Low and rough, his voice sounded from beside her. "Cassie…"

She liked how his name for her rolled off his tongue.

He took a step closer, reached out, not for her, but for a stray thread on the sleeve of her t-shirt, his fingers brushing her arm. The contact was electric, a jolt of pure, unadulterated awareness that made her forget to breathe. "I know we have a deal."

She nodded.

"But the bed is… big enough. I'll stay on my side. Promise. Okay?"

Her head barely managed a nod. "Of course. Yes. Fine."

He gave her a small, lazy smile that could have made her forget her own name, and took a step back. "Jillian put my things in the tallboy dresser. I'll just pop into the bathroom and change if you want to go ahead and unpack. You can have mom's dresser and all the closet space you want."

"Right." She spun around and glanced at the two suitcases someone had placed by the wide dresser. "I, uh, think I'll unpack tomorrow. I'll just fish out my pajamas and toothbrush."

In what felt like only a minute, she'd barely had time to grab what she needed out of the suitcase when Kade appeared in sweatpants and a Don't Tread on Me t-shirt. "Do you have a preferred side of the bed?"

She shook her head and fled to the bathroom, moving slowly, and changed into her own sweats and t-shirt. When she finally emerged, Kade was on the far side of the bed. Hurrying forward, she slid into her own side of the bed, and rolled over to turn off the light.

"Good night, Cassie."

"Good night." Pulling the covers up to her chin. She didn't dare turn around. She hugged the edge of the mattress and wondered what was stranger: waking up married, or going to sleep with her new husband?

CHAPTER SEVEN

Slowly opening her eyes, it took Cassidy a moment to remember why she was waking up in a strange bed, in a strange room. Turning her head quickly, there was no sign of Kade. At least not in bed. Craning her neck, she glanced into the adjoining bathroom. No Kade. What time was it? Eight. Boy, folks sure got up and going early around here. Then again, ranchers pretty much rose and settled in with the chickens. Whatever that meant.

Whipping the covers over to one side, she rose and hurried into the bathroom and dressed for the day. Jeans and sweats seemed about as practical for ranch clothes as she could get. Donning her sneakers, she took a deep breath and made her way downstairs. On the first floor, she followed the scent of coffee and laundry detergent to a spacious utility room off the kitchen.

Alice Sweet stood among a mountain of towels, humming softly as she set aside a folded one. "Good morning, dear. Sleep well?"

"Very well, thank you." It wasn't entirely a lie. Once she'd finally fallen asleep, she'd slept like the proverbial baby. "Let me help with that." Cassidy reached for a towel.

"Nonsense. You're still a newlywed," Alice gently shooed her hand away, "and newlyweds aren't supposed to work. My brood are coffee drinkers. Would you like a cup while I whip up some breakfast for you?"

"No, thank you. I'm not very hungry this morning." No point telling the woman she preferred tea for breakfast.

Kade's mother studied her for a long moment, then gave a resigned nod. "Well, if you're looking for Kade, he and Rachel are out in the barn."

"Thank you. I'll go…" She hesitated. Go what?

Lifting the folded towels in her arms, Alice Sweet chuckled. "I'm sure he's anxious to see you. Go on."

"Yes." She had no idea if Kade wanted to see her or not, but she was too nervous to hang out with a woman who thought her son had fallen madly in love and was anxious to see his bride. Passing a fruit bowl on the counter, Cassidy grabbed an apple and headed outside.

The morning sky was that cloudless shade of blue she was starting to associate with Texas. She had no idea why Montana was called Big Sky country. From where she stood, Texas had to have the corner on the big sky market. Forcing herself to put one foot in front of the other, almost at the open door, a knocking sound caught her ear. Slowing her steps, she strained to listen. By the time she reached the doorway, both Kade and Rachel were standing side by side, staring in her direction.

"I wondered who had Boots all worked up." Kade smiled.

The horse she'd met last night had her head over the stall door, shaking and making funny noises, and Cassidy was pretty sure that knocking sound was the horse's hoof hitting the door.

Holding a clipboard, Rachel smiled. "Looks like you've made a friend."

"Can I give her an apple? I saw it on the counter and I've heard that horses like apples."

"Sure." Kade nodded. "Not that you need to bribe her, but feed her apples and she'll be your friend for life."

Approaching slowly, Cassidy pulled the apple from her pocket. "Hey, girl."

Boots's soft lips found the apple. Cassidy held her hand flat, smiling as the massive animal gently retrieved it, crunched away, and then moved her lips, tickling Cassidy's palm, making sure she'd not left any morsel behind.

The horse nudged her and Cassidy began stroking her neck. "Such a sweet girl."

"Especially when you give her what she wants," Rachel called out without looking up from her clipboard. Kade stood beside her frowning at stacks of feed bags.

"I just don't get it." Rachel's tone held a hint of frustration. "The numbers aren't adding up."

Cassidy stayed where she was, stroking Boots's soft nose. She didn't mean to eavesdrop, but the barn was a cavern of sound, and their conversation carried. They talked of feed bags, consumption rates, and herd sizes. It was a language she didn't speak, a world she didn't know, but the core of their problem was something she understood intimately: numbers. She let them talk for another minute, her own mind quietly running the calculations, turning the variables over. Gently patting the horse's neck, she whispered, "I'll be right back," and the way the animal barely dipped her head made Cassidy think the mare actually understood. Slowly moving closer, she glanced at the papers. "What's going on?"

Rachel gestured to the feed bags. "Preston's in town dealing with the feed supplier, and we're trying to figure out our supply levels. We've got this new delivery; plus what's left from last month, and..." she trailed off, looking at the stacks like they might rearrange themselves into something more comprehensible.

Kade tapped his pencil against the notepad. "Trying to calculate if we have enough to get us through till the next scheduled delivery. Consumption rate per head, weight variations between full and partial bags..." He scrubbed a hand through his hair. "I don't know, it looks like we have enough for maybe two weeks? Three?"

Cassidy's eyes moved across the barn, counting stacks automatically, her brain already categorizing: full bags here, three quarters there, that one's maybe half. She'd been doing it since she walked in, not even consciously, the same way she used to track cards at the table. Looking down at the notes, she pointed to one set of numbers. "Is this how many head of cattle?"

Kade nodded. "And these are the horse numbers."

Cassidy walked closer to the stacks. Full bags were easy, she'd seen the labels—fifty pounds each. The partial ones took a bit more estimation, but her brain had always been good at that. Weight, volume, the slight sag of a bag that was two-thirds full versus half. She looked at the notes, at the scratched-out calculations, the numbers that didn't quite add up because they were trying to do too many variables at once. Her finger traced down the page. "Is that your consumption rate? Twenty-eight pounds per head per day?"

"Yeah. Average, anyway."

The math assembled itself in her head like cards falling into place. "You've got nineteen and a half days' worth. Twenty if you stretch it. You'll need to reorder in about two weeks to be safe, just in case there are delivery issues."

Lifting her gaze, she spotted Kade and Rachel staring at her, jaws slightly open, eyes round as golf balls.

The barn went quiet. Even the animals seemed to stop their movements at Cassie's mathematical analysis. On the fly analysis. Kade turned slowly. "Come again?"

"Nineteen and a half days." She pointed to the full bags. "Those are sixteen days right there if they're all fifty-pound bags. The partial ones add another three and a half, maybe four if you're conservative with feeding. Twenty days if you cut back slightly on the horses' grain and supplement with more hay."

Her eyes still perfectly round, Rachel snapped her jaw shut, then opened it again. "You just calculated that? In your head?"

Cassidy shrugged, her gaze lowering to the floor before lifting her head again. "It's just math. Multiplication and addition."

"Just math," Kade muttered, remembering she'd mentioned something about being able to remember numbers, but calculating on the fly was more than remembering numbers.

"We've been working on this for almost an hour." Rachel looked down at the paper, scribbled some numbers, glanced at the bags and then back at her. "I think you're right."

"I count cards," she said simply, as if that explained everything. And maybe it did. "This is easier. The variables don't change as fast."

Rachel handed her the clipboard. "You'd better write this down for Preston. I'm sure he's going to like your numbers better than anything we came up with."

Cassidy took the notepad and pencil, wrote out the calculations, showing her work in neat columns. Days of supply, consumption rates, the buffer for unexpected needs. "Is this okay?"

"Okay?" Kade shook his head. "It's amazing." Before he realized what he was doing, he'd pulled her against him and gave her a hard peck on the lips, then surprised by his own movements, took a quick step back. "Thank you. You've been an enormous help."

"Any time." Her cheeks blushed light pink and he had to resist the urge to kiss her thank you again.

"Don't think we're not going to take you up on that," Rachel shot back, shoving the clipboard at her brother. "Now that this little dilemma is resolved, I'm heading back to the house. I have a few calls to make and pray I don't have to go into the office."

Kade set the paperwork aside. Cassie had already turned and walked back by Boots's side. "She likes you."

"I like her." She offered her first sincere smile of the day.

Funny how a city girl could relate so easily to Boots. Usually, the massive size of working horses would scare the dickens out of city folk, but Cassie just took to Boots. "Have you been around horses before?"

She shook her head.

"Well, you could have fooled me. You knew she'd like apples, you knew to keep your palm flat. You're standing in just the right spot so she can see you and doesn't get spooked. And there's no hesitancy in your touch."

"I remember things."

"Like counting cards."

She nodded.

"I have a feeling I'm going to have to be on my toes around you."

Her head snapped around, eyes wide.

The sudden shift in her expression had him chuckling. "Nothing bad, but I've never known anyone quite like you."

"I hope that's a good thing. Wouldn't want to get kicked out before the year is up."

"Not a chance, even if you couldn't do math." His gaze followed the tender way her fingers stroked the horse. "Would you like to take her for a ride? A short one?"

Now her eyes widened not with fear or concern but with excitement. "Can I?"

"Yeah. Let me show you how to saddle her up." Focusing on the task at hand, he pulled a thick, woven blanket from a rack, the familiar weight of it settling in his hands. "First things first, the saddle blanket." Placing it high on Boots's withers, he slid it back into place. "You want to ensure the horse's coat lays flat and smooth underneath."

Listening intently, she nodded. Her attention absolute, her movements mirroring his when he removed the blanket and gave it to her to try again. There was no wasted motion. No hesitation.

"Excellent. You did good."

"I watched you."

That she had. He was beginning to understand just how much she could learn by merely watching. Not just cards and numbers, but apparently, horses too.

Next came the saddle. She hadn't flinched at the heavy weight, just positioned herself and swung it onto the horse's back with a surprising, efficient grace.

"All right, now the cinch." He moved to the other side, keeping his voice low and steady, and talked her through the process of tightening the leather straps, his hands occasionally brushing against hers in the tight space. Each touch an accident, a necessity of the lesson, but it sent a jolt of awareness through him nonetheless.

With Boots and his mount saddled, they led the horses out into the sunlit paddock. "Here we go." He cupped his hands to give her a leg up. She placed her foot in his hands without a second thought. A simple act of trust that struck him as anything but simple. With his gentle boost, she settled into the saddle like she'd been riding her whole life. Covering her hands with his, he positioned her fingers on the reins. "If you hold them loosely, she'll move forward. If you pull them to your left, she'll turn left. If you pull to the right—"

"She'll turn right," she repeated with a knowing smile.

"Guess that was pretty obvious."

Grinning, she nodded. "And pulling both together at the same time will tell her to stop."

"Exactly." He frowned, wondering how she'd figured that one out on her own.

"I used to love reruns of *Gunsmoke*. Whenever the horses came to a galloping stop, you could see that the riders were tugging hard on the reins. They also kicked with their heels to make the horses go, and sometimes slapped the reins from side to side to make them run faster."

"Yeah, well," he rubbed his hand along the back of his neck, "that pretty much covers it. But with Boots, the slightest tap of your heels will get her going faster." He glanced down at her shoes. "Which reminds me, we'll have to see if any of Jillian or Rachel's boots will fit you until we get you your own pair. The last thing anyone wants to do is step in something unpleasant if you're not wearing proper footwear."

Her knowing nod told him she understood exactly what he meant.

Turning to his own mount, he swung up and on, and took the reins. Keeping his pace slow as he led the horse in a wide circle around the enclosure. He watched her, the initial stiffness in her posture giving way to a relaxed, easy rhythm in perfect synchronization with the horse's movement. A genuine, unadulterated smile lit up her face. A look of pure, childlike joy that made his own chest want to puff out with pride at helping put that grin on her beautiful face.

"This is amazing." Her gaze swept over the sprawling pastures.

"It is." In that moment, bathed in the warm Texas sun, she didn't look like a blackjack dealer from Vegas. She looked like she belonged right here. And wasn't that food for thought.

CHAPTER EIGHT

Standing in her new bedroom, the one Cassidy shared with Kade, she unpacked the last of her suitcase. This morning had been way more enjoyable than she'd ever expected. Who knew horses could be so much fun. She almost wished Boots could talk. Cassidy suspected that animal was privy to all sorts of shenanigans the Sweet children had been a part of. The more interesting thing was that she really wanted to know what Kade had been like as a kid.

"Mom's making dinner but she reminded me there's a concert in the park tonight." Kade leaned against the doorframe. "Might be a nice outing, if you're up for it—especially if you like hot dogs."

Closing the drawer, she turned. "A concert?"

"Local band. Nothing fancy, but a good chunk of the town usually turns out. There's plenty of vendors, popcorn, sodas, pretzels. That sort of thing." Lips pressed tightly, she was beginning to recognize when he was couching his words for something he considered important. "We'd be seen together. As a couple. Are you ready for that?"

The question hung in the air. Was she ready? To be on display, to play the role of his wife in front of everyone? Curiosity won over hesitation. She wanted to see more of Honeysuckle, wanted to understand this place that meant so much to him. "Yeah. I think so."

"You sure? We can skip it if you're not comfortable."

"I'm sure." She did her best to flash a self-assured smile and prayed her knees didn't knock. "What time?"

"Music starts at seven. We should leave in about twenty minutes."

"Your mom won't mind if we skip dinner?"

He shrugged. "It was her idea. I think she doesn't want you to feel isolated out here in the middle of nowhere."

"Isolated?" Cassidy shook her head. "Are you kidding? This place is awesome."

"Really?" His face reminded her of a little boy who'd just been told for the first time that the tooth fairy would come and leave him money under his pillow. "And here I was worried I'd find you up here repacking and ready to catch the first flight back to Las Vegas."

"Not on your life. I'm yours for the year." Her words registered a moment too late and she felt heat creep up her neck. "I mean…"

He chuckled and pushing away from the frame, held up his hand. "I know what you meant." Stepping into the room, he stopped a few feet away from her. "If we're going to do this for months, you can't keep worrying I'm going to misconstrue whatever you say."

She bobbed her head.

"You're going to have to trust me a little bit."

"But I do." How could he think she'd have come if she didn't?

"Then we're off to do the town." A smile spread across his face and put every unsettled nerve at ease.

The ride into Honeysuckle didn't take near as long as she thought. In town, the evening air was warm and fragrant with the scent of cut grass and popcorn and other savory smells she couldn't quite pinpoint.

Hyper-aware of Kade's hand resting lightly on the small of her back as he guided her through the sea of blankets and lawn chairs, she reminded herself to breathe.

"Relax," he murmured against her ear. "Just be yourself."

"Myself. Got it."

"This is going to be easy. Operation Convince the Town is officially underway." His designating their foray into town with a mission name made her smile now the same as it had when he'd first mentioned it.

The band started—country with a rock edge, fiddle and

guitar mixing in a way that was distinctly Texas. She found herself swaying slightly, Kade's arm a warm, steady comforting presence at her waist. Suddenly, the light pressure against her back shifted, his whole body went stiff.

"Deep breath, soldier, you look like you're about to breach a hostile compound."

He let out a short, surprised laugh, the sound of a low rumble that vibrated through her, then whispered into her ear, "Threats acquired."

Her gaze followed his, landing on two women holding court on a picnic blanket. One of them glittered from head to toe, a human disco ball catching the last rays of the setting sun. "Let me guess. The bling queen?"

"Mildred McEntire in the flesh." He gave the woman a friendly wave and redirected Cassidy toward a spot near the back, under the sprawling branches of live oak trees. "The woman she's with is Iris Hathaway. Telegraph, telephone, and tell Iris. Between her and Mildred, if anyone in town didn't know we're an item, they will in a few minutes."

That had Cassidy giggling. "Got it. So small-town stories are true."

"Every word."

The local band on the gazebo stage was surprisingly good, their music a comfortable, easy rhythm that seemed to settle over the crowd. For a moment, watching families and couples relax in the twilight, she let herself forget they were on display.

"You weren't kidding." She lifted her chin toward well-lit corn hole courts at the edge of the park, where a game was still in full swing.

Smiling, he shook his head. "It's a requirement for residency."

She laughed, a bright, clear sound that did wonders to finish unraveling the nervous knots that had been tightening in her gut all day. "I'm sensing you're not entirely joking."

"Only a little." He turned to her, his blue eyes sparkling with a challenge. "Want to give it a try?"

Staring into the distance at the group playing, she shrugged. "How hard can it be?"

He led her over to an empty court and explained the rules with a mock seriousness that made her smile. She listened, her mind not just hearing the words but seeing the angles, calculating the trajectory, absorbing the simple, elegant geometry of the game. Her first few throws were decent, landing solidly on the board. His were better. Next turn she took a breath, adjusted her stance, and pictured the arc in her mind. She tossed the bag. It sailed through the air in a perfect, smooth curve, landing dead center and sliding directly into the hole. "And that," she dusted her hands off with a triumphant grin, "is what we call a comeback."

It pleased her more than she could say that his smile was genuine. So many men in her life had been intimidated by the way her mind worked, and the things she could do because of it. This was… nice.

The game and the concert wound down at just about the same time. She wouldn't have minded if they'd both lasted a little longer.

His hand found hers, his fingers lacing through hers in a way that felt surprisingly natural. "How about a beer at the Whiskey Moon?"

The suggestion came as if he'd read her mind. For reasons she couldn't explain, that made her truly happy. "I think I'd like that."

"You think?" Why did that single word bother him so?

Her head tipped and her smile softened. "Correction. I know I'd like that."

Those few words made him happier than they should have. "Then the Whiskey Moon it is."

For as long as he could remember, the favorite town tavern hadn't changed much. Probably had looked exactly like this before he was even born. Scarred floors, a long bar with mismatched stools, a jukebox in the corner, and pool tables under a lamp that had seen better decades welcomed them. The low murmur of conversation from the handful of patrons at the bar was a nice change from the earlier concert crowd.

Letting go of her hand and moving it to the small of her back, he guided her to a small, two-top table in the back, away from the main flow of traffic but with a clear view of the two pool tables that dominated the far side of the room.

A waitress appeared. "Kade Sweet. I heard you were back in town. It's been forever."

"It's nice to be home."

"I hear congratulations are in order."

Nodding, his smile seemed to tug hard at his cheeks. Mildred and Iris were even better than he remembered at spreading breaking news. "Thank you. This is Cassie."

"Nice to meet you," the two said at the same time.

"So," the woman asked, "what can I get you?"

"Two Shiner Bocks." He turned to Cassie, realizing he probably should have asked before ordering the favorite Texas beer. "Okay with you?"

She nodded and smiled demurely. A man could get used to that.

"Coming right up." The waitress turned and stopping at a couple of other tables on her way, headed for the bar.

Together they took in the crowd.

Cassie began tapping her fingers to a familiar tune. "Did you come here a lot?"

"Often enough. At least once we were legal. In a town this small, it's kind of hard to sneak in with fake IDs."

"I can see where that would be a challenge."

"What about you? Did you sneak into bars before you were legal?"

She shook her head. "When you're in the system you turn eighteen and are shown the front door. Doesn't leave a person with a lot of time or money to play around."

That made his heart squeeze. Some of his best memories came from the crazy things he and his friends did between high school and joining the Army. "I'm sorry."

"Why? It's not your fault."

He shrugged. What more could he say? She was right. It wasn't his fault or his responsibility and yet it bothered him more than he could say to think she had a less than ideal childhood.

The waitress returned with two beers and two glasses. Another table called her over and turning on her heel, she scurried over.

Kade ignored the glass and grabbed the long neck bottle, his gaze drifting to the pool tables. "You play?"

She shook her head.

"Want to learn?"

Her gaze shifted to the two tables, one empty, and taking a second to consider, bobbed her head. "Sure."

They moved to the open table. Quickly, he explained the rules, then racked the balls, the sharp, solid clack a satisfying sound. She chose a cue stick with a surprising amount of care, testing its weight and balance. He watched, fascinated, as the blackjack dealer's focus returned, her gaze sharp, analytical.

Positioning himself against the table, he broke, the balls scattering in a chaotic spray. It was a decent break, but nothing dropped. He stepped back. "Your shot."

She leaned over the table, her movements fluid and precise. She wasn't just hitting the ball; she was calculating, seeing the angles, planning her next three moves. He found himself not watching the game, but watching her. The way she bit her lower lip in concentration. The stray wisp of dark hair that had escaped her ponytail and brushed against her cheek. The quiet confidence in her stance.

"You're doing it again."

Leaning over the table, cue stick resting on her fingers, she raised her gaze to meet his. "Doing what?"

"Turning everything into math."

She lined up her next shot, sank it clean, then straightening, turned to face him. "Is that a problem?"

"No." He smiled as she circled the table, analyzing her next shot. "It's impressive as hell."

By the third game, she was beating him. Not by much, but enough. She sank three stripes in a row before finally missing a tricky bank shot. She straightened up, a look of mock frustration on her face. "Your turn."

He missed an easy shot, the cue ball scratching into a side pocket.

"Tough break." She tried to sound empathetic, but the twinkle in her eye told him she was enjoying whooping him.

The jukebox played something slow. For a moment, Kade considered asking her to dance in the small space near the corner. But that felt too intimate, too real. Instead, he finished his beer. "One more game?"

"You sure you want another loss?"

They played another couple of rounds and then to his chagrin, the morning came early. "We should probably head back."

Nodding, she placed her cue on the wall rack and accepted his proffered hand as though it was the most natural thing in the world. To his surprise, after only a couple of days, it did indeed feel natural to him.

The drive home was quiet. When they pulled up to the dark house, Kade turned off the engine and twisted to face her. "We did good tonight. I was a little surprised more folks didn't ask a bunch of probing questions, but I think we looked so natural, they didn't see the need."

"I sure hope so."

He helped her out of the car, and mindful of the possibility his mother might be waiting for them, took hold of her hand and didn't let go until they crossed the threshold of the master bedroom.

Tonight, getting ready for bed flowed more casually. There was still an awkward air to the room, but better than last night. Same as the night before, Kade was the first to change and climb into bed. When Cassie climbed in beside him, even though it seemed an ocean away, he wished he could remember more of their one true night together. On the other hand, it was probably better he didn't.

"Kade?"

"Yeah?"

"I had fun tonight. Real fun."

"Me too."

"I'm glad. Good night."

"Night." Rolling over to face the window, he closed his eyes and wondered how he was supposed to sleep?

CHAPTER NINE

Approaching the Sweet home, Clint felt a bit like a stray mutt about to stain the pristine home with his presence. He always felt that way around Alice Sweet and her family. He wished he could have done more to help them after that sleazebag of a foreman and his ranch hands swindled them out of almost everything they had.

Shaking his head, he thought back to the day Ray hired him. It had been rough finding work with his record. Ex-cons everywhere had a tough time getting a fresh start, but he'd been particularly worn down. When all Ray had to say was "everyone makes mistakes," Clint had thought he'd stumbled onto the best man on the planet. In return, Clint had worked doubly hard to repay the foreman, only to slowly notice a few anomalies and then one day, everyone was gone, along with all the new equipment that had been purchased. It hadn't taken much to connect the dots. He'd been hired because the thieving foreman thought an ex-con would fit right in with the rest of the gang. The irony of it all was that the same foreman was probably one of the few people on the planet who knew Clint was a hard-working honest man who would never have…. Shaking his head, he was not going there. Not now. Not today.

Pausing to use the boot scraper, he knocked lightly before entering the home. At the counter Alice Sweet, hunched over, wielded a massive knife as long as the counter space in front of her.

"I could come back."

Alice glanced in his direction. "Tomorrow is Kade and Cassie's seven-day anniversary."

"Day?"

She shrugged. "They had a smaller than small ceremony, no reception, no honeymoon. Didn't seem right to wait a whole year to celebrate." She straightened, stretching her back left then right, before setting the cake she'd just sliced across the middle onto a pile of other cake layers. "I considered waiting a month, but this made sense for Kade's favorite. A seven-layer cream cake."

His gaze shifted from the stack of half cakes on the side to the whole one on her left that was obviously the next one for her to tackle. "I'm guessing you're not using whole cakes to avoid creating the Leaning Tower of Pisa."

Her chuckle made him smile. "Good observation." She pulled the last cake over. "Don't tell me you bake too?"

He came within a flash of telling her that his wife had loved to bake. Instead he merely shook his head, remembering how that woman loved to tinker in the kitchen. The house always smelled of cinnamon, or vanilla, or some combination thereof.

One palm flat on the top of the cake, she slowly sliced through the middle of this last layer. "Preston tells me that we've just about caught up with your back salary."

"Yes, ma'am, but I told you—"

"Don't even go there," she cut him off. "And that's not the reason I asked you to stop by." She set the sliced cake aside. "Apparently, we have enough breathing room that we can hire one full-time ranch hand for you."

"For me?"

She spun about to face him. "Well, for us, but since you've been doing the bulk of the full-time work around here with sporadic help from my children and me, I think— we think—you should be the one to interview the candidates."

He knew his eyes had to be bugging out of his head. He'd worked here less than a year. Was a lowly ranch hand. He had no business making those kinds of choices for the family. "I don't—"

Her hand shot up, and once again she cut him off. "And you might as well know, you'll be made foreman." And just like that, a huge smile spread across her face at the exact moment her arms crossed in front of her, practically daring him to argue.

A smile slowly teasing the corners of his mouth, he slapped his hat against his thigh and lifted his gaze to meet hers. "Thank you, ma'am. I won't let you down."

"You haven't yet. I doubt you ever will."

He had to ask himself, would she think that way if she knew the truth about his past?

"I still think it would have been more fun on horseback." Cassidy hopped out of the four-wheeler.

"Trust me, when we're done working the line, you're going to be darn happy that we can get back to the ranch quickly on a cushioned seat and not a leather saddle."

"If you say so." Of course she believed Kade, but she'd lived in too many households with too many young boys, not to want to give them a little grief along the way. Even someone as nice as Kade. And the man was very nice. Of course, she'd thought so from the first moment she'd noticed him and he'd come to her rescue. Had she not felt totally safe and secure with the man she'd known less than twenty-four hours, she would never have agreed to this crazy scheme. Which, if she were being honest, didn't seem so crazy anymore.

"You're smiling." Kade hefted a toolbox out of the back of the four-wheeler and stood there staring at her. "What's got you so happy?"

Her gaze scanned from left to right. "Who wouldn't be happy out here?"

"A lot of people," he sort of scoffed before walking the tool box over to the broken fence line. "Especially folks raised in the city and used to a gas station on every corner and a shopping mall within walking distance."

She shrugged. "Convenience is nice, but it doesn't compete with this beautiful sky and warm sunny days."

"Wait till winter hits and all you can see is miles and

miles of snow."

"Snow's pretty."

Kade chuckled. "You always find the bright side of things. Don't you ever just want to rant?"

"Sure, but what's the point?" She'd spent plenty a night crying about where she lived, or what she had to deal with, or that last year in the system wondering how she was going to survive on her own, but none of her tears changed anything. Walking behind him, she came to a stop at the downed post. Together, they held it up as Kade used his clippers to cut off the damaged wire and restrung the post.

If she did say so herself, she thought she was improving at the fence line. She'd fumbled too often the first day they went out to help, and the second day she'd cut her fingers up, even with gloves. Today, she thought she was doing darn good.

"You're smiling again." This time he had a grin almost as wide as hers.

Shrugging, she met his gaze. "I think I'm getting better at helping."

"No thinking. You are."

She shifted for a better grip on the post. "Mathematical things come pretty easily to me, but I've never had to work much with my hands. It's nice. Though my back doesn't always agree."

Looking up, he frowned at her. "Maybe we should call it an early day. I can get Clint to help tomorrow, or one of my brothers."

"No." She shook her head firmly. "We're almost done. I can handle it."

"Stubborn," he muttered, though the corner of his mouth twitched in a smile. He went back to stretching a new length of wire, the rhythmic creak of the fence stretcher a familiar sound in the quiet afternoon. Cassidy held the post steady. She liked this. The simplicity of the work, the tangible result, the easy, comfortable silence between them. She was so focused on the task that she didn't notice it at first. It was Kade's sudden, absolute stillness that broke the spell. His body went rigid, his gaze fixed on a spot on the ground just a few feet to her left.

"Don't move," he said, his voice a low, deadly calm.

Her own gaze dropped. Coiled in the grass was a rattlesnake, its head raised, the dry, chilling buzz of its tail cutting through the silence. Cassidy froze, her heart leaping into her throat. Before she could even process a coherent thought, his hand dropped to his right boot, and a small, dark handgun appeared in his grip. Kade's movements were a blur of deadly efficiency. The shot echoed across the open land, and the snake grew instantly still and quiet, its head splattered across the ground. For a long moment, no one moved. Cassidy's knuckles were white where she gripped the fence post.

"You okay?" His voice steady, Kade's eyes scanned the ground around them.

Her throat too tight for words, she could only nod. Silently, he returned the weapon to its ankle holster. She'd known there was a rifle on the vehicle, but had been clueless that he also had a gun on him. "Do you always wear that?"

"The gun?" He nodded, gesturing with his chin toward the now-still snake. "This is Texas. You'd be surprised how many folks have a license to carry. Add to that this is ranch country where you never know what critter is going to come along." He nudged the snake with the tip of his boot. "Plus, my military training… well, you can count on most of us carrying. My sisters included."

Cassidy's mind flashed to the brief, terrifying moment she'd felt so utterly vulnerable. And then to Kade's instant, lethal response. It wasn't just a habit for him; it was a part of who he was. The protector. The soldier. And in that moment, she had never been more grateful for it.

He offered her a small, reassuring smile. "Let's finish up here. I think you've earned that cushioned seat back to the ranch."

★

The sound of the shower shutting off pulled Kade from his thoughts. The bathroom door opened, steam billowing out. Cassidy emerged in clean jeans and an untucked button-down shirt. Her hair still damp, twirled into a bun at the back of her head, she looked like an angel.

"Your turn." She moved toward the dresser.

"In a minute." Holding a small tin of salve in one hand, he pointed to the bed with the other. "Take off your shirt and lie down on your stomach."

Her eyes went wide as saucers.

Suppressing a smile, he shook his head, despite the heat creeping up his neck. "For your back. This salve will help with the soreness."

"Oh." The single syllable came out small. "Of course." She hesitated only a moment before inching toward the bed, standing in front of him, her back to him, she unbuttoned the shirt and let it slide off her shoulders then tossed it onto the bed as she climbed onto the mattress and lay down.

Kade settled beside her, warming the salve between his palms. The first touch made her flinch. "Cold?"

"A little."

He worked the salve into the tight muscles along her spine, feeling the knots from hours of fence work. Her skin was warm beneath his hands, and he tried to focus on the task, not the way her breath caught when he found a particularly sore spot.

"Dad swore this stuff could cure anything. Charley horse—the salve. Sprained muscle—the salve. Twisted something or other—the salve. I'd swear if he'd had any, he would have used it for warts and ulcers."

The bedspread against her face muffled her laugh. "Windex."

"Excuse me?"

"*My Big Fat Greek Wedding*. The father used Windex to fix everything. It was a running gag throughout the movie."

"Never saw it."

Shoving up on one arm, she turned her head to glance at him from over her shoulder. "You're kidding me?"

He shook his head. "Nope."

"Oh, you have to see it. It's a classic right up there with *My Cousin Vinny*."

"That one I've seen." His fingers continued to press and rub at a particularly stubborn knot.

Easing herself back onto the bed, she winced at the pressure before sighing. "I guess I'm more out of shape than I thought." They were quiet for a moment, just the sound of his hands moving across her skin, the rhythm of her breathing. "In foster care nobody touched you unless they had to. Medical checks, moving you from house to house. It was all… functional."

Why did those words hurt his heart? Children should remember hugs, and laughter and mothers kissing away the pain when you fell out of a tree and scraped your knee. "What happened to your parents?"

The silence hung so long, he wished that he could take the words back. How stupid could he be?

"I don't remember them very well. I guess, not at all really. I mostly remember the memory but not the people."

He continued to massage her tired muscles. Even though he'd loosened most of the knots, for some reason he wasn't ready to lose this connection.

"I was five when my parents were killed in a car accident. The babysitter took care of me for a short time while authorities tried to find any relatives, but they couldn't. My first home lasted almost four years. Mrs. Winston was really nice. At least I remember her that way, but then she got very sick. Her son explained that she couldn't care for any of us anymore."

"Any of you?"

"There were three of us. Susie was a year older than me and Nancy a year younger. It was nice to have sort of sisters. For a little while." She heaved a deep sigh. "It actually felt like a home, like life was…normal. I had thought that was going to be my forever home. Next house wasn't too bad, but then my friend Penny got moved, or maybe she went back with her parents, not really sure, but I think that's when I learned not to get too attached to anyone or anything."

His mind wandered back to the lack of knick-knacks or personal belongings in her apartment—not a single memento worth bringing with her. Things were making more sense. His chest tightened and his heart pinched. Now he was going to do the same thing to her again. Give her a family for a year, then take it away from her. In his entire life, had he ever felt like such a heel?

CHAPTER TEN

The rhythmic thwack of an axe splitting wood was the only sound in the crisp Saturday morning air. Kade set another log on the block, swung, and felt a satisfying jolt as the wood split cleanly in two. He'd been at it since dawn, working through the restlessness that had settled in his bones since last night. Rubbing salve on Cassidy's back had been a mistake. Not the act itself—he could tell by the way she moved this morning that it had helped. The mistake had been the easy intimacy of it, the quiet murmur of her voice as she told him about her past, and the gut-wrenching realization that this temporary arrangement was setting her up for another loss. He set another piece of firewood in place.

"You're going to chop through the whole wood pile before breakfast if you keep that up."

He turned. Cassidy stood a few feet away, two steaming mugs in her hands, a small, knowing smile on her face. She was dressed in jeans and one of his old, worn flannel shirts, the sleeves rolled up to her elbows. On her, it looked better than it ever had on him.

"Figured you could use this." She held a mug out to him.

Setting the axe aside, he accepted the proffered mug, the ceramic warm against his calloused hands. *Coffee.* Elixir of the gods. "Thanks." He took a long, grateful sip.

"You were thinking pretty loud out here." Her gaze swept over the growing pile of split wood.

Not trusting himself to speak, he merely grunted in response.

She leaned against the railing of the back porch, sipping

her tea, scanning the distance. Her gaze darted to his between sips. "What's eating you?"

"Nothing."

She shook her head from left to right. "Not buying it."

"Why not?"

"We've been back a week and this is the first time I've seen you chopping wood. Should I mention we're nowhere near winter? Besides, when something's bothering you that little muscle on the right side of your jaw flexes."

The woman had powers of observation that could put the Hubble telescope to shame, but was it actually possible that in only a week she had learned to read him so easily? He'd dated women for months who didn't have a clue what he was thinking or when something had set his nerves on edge—especially when they were the ones tugging on his last nerve.

Taking another sip, he considered his options. Tell her that he was battering his own body as early punishment for the end of the year when he took another home away from her. Maybe tell her that when she hurt, he hurt.

"I've been thinking," she spoke softly over the rim of her cup. "I asked Jillian after supper last night why she carries a gun."

Well, that was interesting.

"She shrugged as if it were the most natural thing in the world, then added, 'if something serious, crazy, or deadly goes down, I don't want to become the helpless victim.'"

He bobbed his head. Defending hearth, home, and yourself was pretty much the Texas mantra.

"Maybe I should learn to shoot." Determination shone in her eyes. "Could you teach me?"

"Why?"

She took another sip of her tea, staring down at the warm brew a moment. "I want to be able to defend the ranch, and your family, if someone…something," she corrected, "came along."

Interesting choice of words. "You're thinking about what Preston said at dinner last night about finding one of the lines ransacked."

Her chin dipped in a single motion. "No one came out and said it, but I could see from the way everyone stiffened and grew serious that at least a few of you think that old foreman or his hands had something to do with it."

He couldn't argue. They did. He was almost willing to stake his career on it. But that wasn't what had his gut churning. This woman was taking on every aspect of the ranch, from working it, to fixing it, and now defending it. Maybe marrying her was the smartest thing he'd ever done.

"Well?"

"All right." Nodding his head, he set his coffee down. "No time like the present."

A bright smile took over her face making her eyes sparkle. Damn, how he loved making her happy.

Retrieving a handgun and ammunition from in the house, he led her out behind the barn. Taking a couple of wooden sawhorses from a nearby storage shed, he set up a little shooting range with oil cans. Next, he went into instructor mode, walking her through the safety protocols, the mechanics of the weapon, the importance of treating every weapon as if it were loaded, and never ever point it at anyone unless you intend to shoot. And with that came the familiar refrain: if you shoot, shoot to kill.

She listened, her focus absolute, her green eyes tracking his every move. Following his instructions, she slipped five rounds into the magazine, set her stance shoulder width apart, brought the sights to the can, and eased the trigger with slow steady pressure. She fired. The can on the far left pinged and jumped off the post. She fired again. The second can flew into the air. A third shot, and the last can disappeared.

A natural. He shouldn't have expected anything less from this amazing woman. Shaking his head, a slow laugh rumbled in his chest. "I married Annie Oakley."

"Hardly." She smiled back. "Beginner's luck."

"Not a chance." He walked over to the sawhorses, placed the cans on top once again, then returning to her side, gave her five more rounds and watched as she readied her stance, set her sights, and one by one sent each oil can flying. "Cassie Barker, you are simply full of surprises."

Pride and joy were both painted on her face. "I did it. I actually did it."

So much for beginner's luck. He bobbed his head, grinning back at her. There was no doubt in his mind that she was going to make one helluva rancher's wife. And why did he suddenly wish more than anything else that this year didn't have to come to an end and he could be that rancher?

Pure, unadulterated triumph bloomed in Cassidy's chest. She lowered the handgun, the weight of it surprisingly solid and manageable in her hands, and stared at the empty sawhorse. She'd done it. She'd actually hit all the targets. Not by chance but every time.

The genuine admiration in Kade's eyes was a heady thing, a warmth that spread through her and settled deep in her bones. In that moment she wasn't a foster kid or a blackjack dealer. She was a woman who could hold her own, a woman who had just impressed a highly trained soldier. And the feeling was ridiculously, wonderfully good. In just a week, she felt more and more comfortable around the family, the house, and the ranch. Who knew this girl born and raised in the city would enjoy tending to horses or fences?

Taking a minute, she slanted a glance in Kade's direction and felt her cheeks tug at the corners of her mouth as an idea rattled around in the back of her mind. "So." She looked to the sawhorses and back. "What say you to a little friendly competition?"

The way Kade's eyes widened followed by a wide grin and full on belly laugh, he bobbed his head and reached for another weapon resting on the barrel beside him. "You're on." Gathering new targets, Kade set up the cans side by side. "Ladies first."

Cassidy took aim, pulled the trigger, and grinned when she made what looked to her like a bull's-eye.

Nodding, Kade marched over to the can, drew a large circle around the shot, then returned to stand beside her. Taking aim, he fired.

This time, Cassidy walked beside him, grinning when Kade lifted the can. His shot was slightly up and left from hers dead center. They did this over and over for the next hour or so. Jostling back and forth for first place.

In the end, Kade beat her by one round. "For someone who has never even held a gun before, I think it's safe to say you can most definitely hit the broadside of a barn."

"You didn't do so bad yourself."

"Gee, thanks." He'd pretty much smiled and laughed the whole time they'd been out in the middle of the field shooting at oil cans. If she had any really good friends to tell this to, they wouldn't believe her. She wasn't all that sure she believed what she'd just done.

"There you are." Garret made his way around the back of the barn. "Mom is setting up for a lunch. She's sent out the call for the whole family to be here."

"What's wrong?" Kade's brows buckled quickly with concern.

Garret shrugged. "No idea what she's up to, but the way she's smiling and whistling, I don't think anything is wrong."

"Okay." Kade nodded. "We'll clean up here and head back."

Keeping her eyes on Garret as he walked away, she noticed Kade still looked worried. "You think something's up?"

"Not sure, but Mom doesn't usually organize big lunches. Dinners for special occasions, yes, but lunches on a Saturday afternoon..." He shrugged. "I'm probably overthinking this. Let's put all this back, and hopefully I'll have time to hit the showers."

"You are a little ripe," she teased.

"Hey..." His expression feigned insult, but his eyes sparkled with amusement.

She merely shook her head and smiled. She really did love hanging out with this man. Her own words caught her off guard. Love. Probably too strong a word—then again, people loved pizza and horseback riding and no one said that would be too strong a word.

"Something wrong?" Carrying the sawhorse in his arms, he paused mid step. "You look like you swallowed a bug."

"No bugs." Though she reflexively swiped at her mouth. "My mind was just wandering." Forcing herself to smile, she backed up a step and grinned. "Bet you can't beat me to the shower!" Turning on her heels, she took off at a fast clip, laughing as he muttered, "no fair" after her.

By the time he'd finished putting their makeshift shooting range away and made it upstairs to their room, she was already coming out of the bathroom, freshly clean and neatly dressed.

"You seriously don't play fair," he teased, ripping his shirt off and tossing it in the corner. "Just so you know, I will get even."

And didn't that just make her want to grin even wider. Kade Sweet certainly knew how to keep a woman on her toes. She liked that—a lot.

"Give me five minutes and we'll go down together."

"Only five minutes?"

Kade shrugged. "I'm in the army. There's no such thing as a long hot shower."

"Got it." She took a seat on the edge of the bed, brushing her hair, checking her watch. She had her doubts about that five minutes.

In exactly four minutes and twenty seconds, the bathroom door opened and Kade stood on the other side, hair still damp, fully clothed, and ready to face his family.

"I'm impressed." Lips pressed tightly together, head cocked to one side, she nodded at him. "Very impressed."

"Come on, wife." He reached for her hand and they walked down the hall and down the stairs. Walking around the house from time to time holding hands, assuming that's what newlyweds would be prone to do, had become second nature to them. It was comfortable.

What had her almost stumbling with surprise was the

title wife. He'd not said that before. Unless you counted the wedding ceremony, she didn't clearly remember.

"There you two are." His mom beamed from where she stood in the kitchen. "Now that we're all here, I have the table set in the dining room."

One by one his siblings and their spouses pushed to their feet, crossed the room, and followed Alice into the massive dining room. When Cassidy and Kade reached the doorway, he stopped short and her head snapped up to see what was going on.

Standing at the end of the table, Alice smiled wider than before, her arm gesturing widely to the centerpiece. A tall, cream-colored cake with a bride and groom topper. "Happy seven-day anniversary!"

Aw, hell. Her fingers tightened around his. If Alice went all out for one week, what would she do for one month, or one year? And then guilt churned in her stomach—or when that year came and ended.

"Close your mouths," Alice chuckled. "You'll catch flies. It's not the same as a real reception, but it will have to do."

Cassie glanced up at Kade and caught him looking at her. His eyes held the same surprise laced with guilt that she felt. Forcing herself to smile and play the delighted newlywed, she tried not to think about how awful she was going to feel in three hundred and fifty-eight days.

CHAPTER ELEVEN

Some mornings were better spent staying in bed. The angry shriek of metal on rock, followed by a sharp crack and a sudden, grinding halt, was a sound Kade knew all too well. He cut the power to the post-hole digger and swore under his breath. He and Clint had been at it since dawn, replacing a section of rotted fence posts in the rocky north pasture, and they'd just hit their third major snag of the morning.

Clint pulled the auger from the hole. The bit was mangled, a twisted piece of useless steel. "Well," Clint said, his voice a dry, dusty rasp, "that was the last spare."

Kade kicked at a loose rock in frustration. "Of course it was." He pulled off his work gloves and wiped a bead of sweat from his forehead with the back of his arm. "All right, I'll head into town."

The walk back to the house was a long, thoughtful one. Except for the irritation of the bit breaking, the last few days had been pleasant and downright peaceful. He and Cassie had fallen into a comfortable routine. Every so often, he almost forgot this marriage was legal but a pretense just the same. Mostly he was reminded at night, after their bedtime ritual, each of them hugging their side of the bed, the need to draw her close and spoon with her had become almost irresistible. It was probably a good thing that he'd be going on temporary duty soon.

Grabbing truck keys from the hook by the back door, Kade stepped fully into the kitchen. "Need anything from town?"

Cassie looked up from where she sat at the table with his mom sorting through seed catalogs.

"Perfect timing." His mom clasped her hands together. "We've picked out some seeds. It's been a while since we did a vegetable garden. I think Cassie here was just the motivation I needed to start up again."

"I'll need a list." His gaze shifted from his mother to Cassie. "Unless…"

Before he could finish his sentence, she was on her feet. "I'll come with you."

It wasn't a question, and he found he didn't want it to be. A month ago, the idea of running errands with someone would seem unnecessary. Now, the thought of her not coming along felt wrong.

"Let me grab my boots."

With the radio set to his mother's favorite oldies station, the ride into town was quick, accompanied by the sound of Cassie humming to the hit tunes of yesteryear. Her voice was low and melodious and he found himself losing track of space and time until the striped red and white awning on Main Street announced that he had arrived at their destination.

He held the door for Cassie, and pointed to the right side of the hardware store. "If things haven't moved around since I was last in here, the seeds should be near the back over there."

Cassie nodded and easily made her way to the seed section.

"Well, isn't this a surprise. Kade Sweet. What brings you in?"

Kade turned to the owner who had been an old man when Kade was a little boy. The guy had to have a portrait of himself up in the attic because he didn't look any older than he had a couple of decades ago. "Just picking up some new auger bits. In the same place?"

The old guy nodded and pointed exactly where Kade had expected to go.

A teenage boy was restocking shelves at the end of the aisle. As Kade scanned the shelves for what he needed, something about the kid just a few feet away caught Kade's attention. Not because of what he was doing, but how he was doing it. The kid moved with mechanical precision, like someone operating on autopilot, his face pale beneath a shock of dark hair. Deep circles shadowed his eyes—not the kind from staying up late playing video games, but the bone-deep exhaustion that came from working too many hours with too little sleep.

Returning his attention to the reason for his errand, he found the auger bits he needed and grabbed a few extra to be safe. Heading over to where Cassie was happily filling a small basket with packets of garden seeds, he took one last look at the kid and wondered what was his story. Was it just a kid out with his friends later than he should be, or was it something else? And when the heck did Kade become an expert on kids? "Find what you two wanted?"

Her head bobbed rapidly, reflecting the enthusiasm in her smile. "All of it, and I thought a few of these flowers might be nice too. I remember reading that marigolds and petunias help deter pests."

"Great idea. Mom will love it."

Pushing to her feet, her gaze stopped at the kid now adjusting items on this aisle. She seemed to study him more thoroughly than he had. The narrow ridge between her brows told him she didn't like what she'd seen any more than he had. Heaving a sigh, she turned to Kade and lifted the basket. "Ready when you are."

The line at the counter was short so it didn't take long for the owner to get to him. "Find everything you need?"

"Yes, sir." Kade stood at Cassie's side as the old guy rang each item up on the ancient push-button register with the speed of a sickly snail. His gaze returning to the kid in yet another aisle, Kade had to ask, "Who's the kid working over there?"

"Jacob? That's Hal and Linda's boy. Hard worker. Wish all teens had his work ethic."

"Know what you mean." Kade flashed a smile and accepted the brown paper bag. "Thanks."

On the street, Cassie walked beside him to the truck, her stride keeping pace with his. "You saw it too."

"Saw it?"

"That kid, Jacob, looked exhausted. Too exhausted for a young boy. Think maybe he works on a ranch and he's just tired from working at the crack of dawn, going to school, then working here afterwards?"

Kade shrugged. "Could be, or he could just be doing whatever it is today's kids like doing when their parents think they're tucked nice and safely in bed."

"Oh," she smiled, "I smell a story. What did young Kade do when his parents thought he was sleeping soundly in bed?"

His grin widened to match hers. "That, my dear lady, is for me to know and you to never find out."

She roared with laughter as she climbed into the truck. He really did love that laugh.

Dinner had been another loud, chaotic, and wonderful affair. Cassidy found herself not just observing the family dynamic anymore, but participating in it. She'd laughed at Garret's story about a disastrous high school science fair project and found herself defending Kade when Jillian teased him about his questionable taste in music as a teenager. By the time Alice declared it was time for dessert on the back porch, Cassidy felt a sense of belonging so profound it was almost frightening.

Now, she sat in one of the old wooden rockers, a slice of apple pie on her lap, listening to the easy rhythm of the family's conversation. The sun had long since set, leaving the sky a deep, velvety black, scattered with a brilliant spray of stars. The air was cool and clean, carrying the sound of distant, gentle lowing of cattle.

One by one, the other couples began to drift away. Once again the mantra early to bed early to rise was more than lip service on a ranch. Now, it was just her and Kade left on the sprawling porch, the comfortable silence settling around them like a warm blanket.

Leaning against the porch railing, his back was to her,

his gaze fixed on the star-dusted horizon. The easy camaraderie of the dinner table had faded, replaced by a quiet, thoughtful stillness that she was beginning to recognize.

"You're thinking again." She set her empty plate aside.

He didn't turn, but she saw his shoulders relax slightly. "Just enjoying the quiet."

She pushed out of her rocker and moved to stand beside him at the railing. The sheer, overwhelming number of stars was breathtaking. In Las Vegas, the city's relentless glow washed out all but the brightest planets. Here, the sky was a living, glittering tapestry. "It's beautiful."

"Yeah." His voice was a low rumble beside her. "Some things you forget when you're away too long. The quiet. The stars." Silent for a moment, he turned his head, his profile silhouetted against the night. "You did good today."

"How hard is it to buy seeds? I'm sure your mom would know about the flower seeds too."

"No, I mean more than starting a new vegetable garden. You fit in like you've always been part of this family."

Though he had no idea that was probably one of the nicest complements she'd ever gotten. "I'm trying my best."

"And nailing it." He smiled at her.

"Your family has been so kind to me. And your mom, in the short time I've been here, treats me as if I were one of her daughters. It's an odd feeling for me."

"I'm sorry." His gaze darkened, he inched closer, taking her hand in his. "If keeping up this pretense for an entire year is going to be too hard for you, we can call it off now. I'll be going on temporary duty soon, you can go back to Vegas, or wherever you want to go, and I'll find a way to tell Mom it just didn't work."

All she could do was blink. Had she totally misread him all this time? Was he wanting to end their deal? Finally, she managed to mutter, "You want me to leave?"

"No." He spoke with a force she'd not heard before. "Not at all. I just know that you were passed from house to house—I won't call any of them a home—and each time it had to hurt. I don't want us to hurt you. I..." He raked his fingers through his hair and paced away from her. "I didn't think what this arrangement might do to you."

It took her a minute to process all his words.

She was still sorting through everything when he turned to pace back in her direction. "I don't ever want to hurt you. Not even a little bit."

Now she got it. "Are you saying you would rather break the deal, lose the money, if staying here was going to make me feel like I was back in the system and about to lose another family?"

Very slowly, he nodded. "Cassie, you matter more to me than money ever could. The ranch will survive. We've come a long way."

She let those words rattle around in her head.

"Cassie? Say something." His voice almost cracked. Had she ever seen him so… vulnerable?

"I like the way you say my name."

Now he was the one staring like a deer in the proverbial headlights. "Cassie?"

"I've always been Cassidy. I like hearing you—and your family—call me Cassie. It makes me feel like… a new person. Like the old Cassidy fell off the face of the earth and Cassie is in her place." She looked off at the stars again. "You know what's strange?"

"What?"

"A month ago, I'd never been on a horse, never shot a gun, never seen a real cow up close. And now…" She gestured to the vast darkness beyond the porch. "Now this feels more like home than anywhere I've ever lived."

Quiet for a long moment, he reached for her hand. "It suits you. All of it."

"You think so?"

"I know so." His smile turned impish. "You're a natural rancher. You've learned everything any of us have shown you. I bet if you wanted to stay on after the year and keep working—for a paycheck, of course—Mom wouldn't object. No one would."

Stay on. Now that was food for thought. Maybe, just maybe, when this year was over she could find someplace in town, stick around. Maybe work here, maybe work somewhere else. Start her life over in Honeysuckle. Wouldn't that be something?

CHAPTER TWELVE

The low thrum of conversation and the familiar twang of a jukebox country song wrapped around Kade as he and Cassie entered the Whiskey Moon. Most of his siblings and their spouses were already there, having claimed a large table that took up most of the back wall of the small local hangout. Garret raised a beer in greeting, a wide grin on his face. It wasn't often they all managed to carve out the same night for a celebration, but between Clint's promotion to foreman, the ranch finally showing a profit, and the sheer miracle of their mother remaining blissfully unaware of their arrangement, a celebration seemed in order.

"Look what the cat dragged in," Carson called out, his own smile easy and relaxed in a way Kade hadn't seen in months.

"Just in time," Jillian added, gesturing to the fresh round of beers the waitress was setting on their table. "We were about to toast to ourselves."

Chairs shifted, making room for the two of them. Sitting side by side, crammed closely together in the tight space, Kade found his hand automatically seeking hers under the table, their fingers lacing together in a gesture that felt less like a performance and more like a simple, necessary truth.

With everyone seated and conversation picking up again, Preston tapped his glass with a piece of cutlery. "I'd like to propose a toast."

Silence fell, at least in this one corner of the bustling establishment, and glasses were raised.

"To turning a corner."

"Hear, hear," voices echoed.

"To Clint and a real ranch hand," Garret added.

"And to Mom never figuring out what we were really up to," Rachel finished, a mischievous sparkle in her eyes.

A chorus of laughter went around the tables. Kade looked at the faces of his siblings, at the incredible women who had joined them, and a profound sense of gratitude washed over him. They had done it. They had pulled the ranch back from the brink.

"And," Preston continued, "to our newest sort-of sister-in-law. With the ranch standing on solid ground for probably the first time since Dad died, and certainly since that idiot foreman bled us all dry, Cassie's help in making rotations and a few other things more efficient, I officially pronounce the Sweet Ranch safe from foreclosure!"

His gaze landed on Cassie. Her eyes wide, her cheeks flushed with embarrassment, a small, genuine smile touched her lips. She belonged here. The thought was no longer a surprise; it was a simple, undeniable fact.

The sound of glasses jostling had Kade turning to the table behind them. Jacob, the kid from the hardware store the other day, was busing the now empty table of six. His movements jerky and rushed, his gaze darted from the table to the bin of dirty glasses and silverware at his side to the patrons dispersed throughout, laughing and drinking, and even dancing. The kid's face screamed fatigue and determination at the same time.

"It's a shame."

Kade turned to face his brother, realizing his gaze was on the same kid.

"Jacob is working harder than the rest of the staff combined."

"Must want that new car pretty badly." Rachel had followed her brother's gazes.

"Doubt it." Garret shook his head, sighed, and took a short sip of his drink. "I'm guessing it has more to do with his sister."

Taking one quick glance around the room, the kid seemed almost nervous before hauling the refuse from the table across the place and into the kitchen.

Facing his brother again, Kade reached for his drink. "He seems more stressed than any teen should be. More stressed than someone working to pay for a car or some other trinket. What's the deal?"

"Emily has some spine disorder. Poor kid has had to wear a brace for as long as I can remember. It has to be miserably uncomfortable for her."

"And don't forget expensive," Rachel added. "The way kids grow, those custom fit suckers have to be redone every so often." She sighed and shook her head. "I hate to admit it but I think you may be right. I forgot that I'd heard Jacob's dad is working nights now at the fertilizer plant."

"Can I get anyone another round?" Their waitress stood at one end of the table, an empty tray under her arm. One by one, she scribbled requests on a pad and then smiled up at them. "Got it. Be right back."

The conversations flowed and Kade couldn't help but think how right all of this felt. How much he missed his family. He loved serving his country. He truly believed what he did made a difference in the world, but he'd never missed all of this as much as he did right now. His gaze shifted to Cassie, chatting with Jillian and laughing at something she'd just said. Maybe it wasn't just the ranch and his siblings that were missing in his life.

"Here we go." The waitress appeared looking a bit more harried, her smile buried under the slightest of scowls.

"Everything okay, Kat?" His sister must have noticed the change in disposition.

"Oh, yeah, sorry." The woman forced a smile. "Must be a full moon or something. We seem to be overrun tonight with cheap tippers. I mean, I know times are tough for everyone, but still." She heaved a sigh, and shaking her head slightly, forced a wider smile. "I forgot your Shiner, I'll be right back."

Spinning on her heel, the waitress hurried back to the bar, pausing a moment to deal with another table.

"I know how she feels." Cassie's eyes were following the woman. "When you're on your own, no real skills, so to speak, no chance for an annual bonus that will pad the down payment fund, no hopes of a key to the executive washroom, it can be tough."

Still holding her hand, he gave it a quick squeeze. Nothing about what she'd just said sat well with him, and everything in him wanted to make sure she never felt that way again. The only problem: what was he going to do about it?

Cassie's insides were still aflutter thinking about the wonderful toast that Preston had made, giving her more credit than she deserved. Pride filled her chest to the point of bursting. Never in her life had she been held in such high esteem by anyone.

The jukebox shifted from an upbeat George Strait number to something slower, softer—an old Alan Jackson ballad that seemed to quiet the room. Couples drifted toward the small dance floor, bodies swaying in the dim light. The evening had flowed like the beer, easy and warm, making it almost possible to forget that this wasn't actually her family, that her place among them had an expiration date.

Kade's hand, still holding hers under the table, gave a gentle squeeze. When she turned to him, his eyes held a question.

"Dance with me?"

Her throat tightened at the unexpected invitation. They'd danced before, on that neon-drenched street in Vegas, a performance for no one but themselves. This felt different—intentional, intimate. She nodded, unable to find her voice.

Kade led her to the dance floor, his fingers threaded through hers, the warmth of his palm against her skin a grounding presence. When he turned to face her, drawing her into his arms, the world condensed to just this moment, just this man. One hand settled on the small of her back, a firm, warm pressure, the heat of it seeping through the thin fabric of her shirt. His other hand held hers, his thumb drawing slow, idle circles over her knuckles. They were dancing closer than was strictly necessary, closer than they'd been since that night she couldn't fully remember. They moved slowly across the floor, finding their rhythm without effort.

With every step, she was hyper-aware of everything: the solid feel of his chest so close to hers, the faint, clean scent of his soap, the way his breath stirred the hair at her temple as he leaned in slightly. The pretend walls she'd been trying so hard to maintain were dissolving, melting away with every heartwarming beat of the old tune. This wasn't an act. This feeling, this dizzying, terrifying, wonderful feeling, was very real.

She risked a glance up at him and found him already watching her, his expression serious, intense. The laughter was gone from his eyes, replaced by a raw vulnerability that mirrored her own. The rest of the bar, his family, the music—it all faded away, leaving only the two of them. They moved in slow circles, her body fitting against his with a rightness that frightened her. This wasn't part of their arrangement, this warmth spreading through her chest, this feeling of coming home. She hadn't agreed to this part. And yet, she wouldn't change her mind for all the tea in China. No, for now, for tonight, she was simply going to lean into this mountain of a man and accept the gift God had given her for however many more days it was meant to be. Even if it meant breaking her heart when it came time to leave.

"Well, look at that." Grinning from ear to ear, Rachel pointed at the dance floor with her chin.

"At what?" Garret shifted to face his sister, his gaze following hers. "The dance floor?"

Rolling her eyes, Jillian shook her head, then playfully smacked her brother. "Not the dance floor. The dancers."

The way their brother focused, eyes narrowed, Rachel hoped he was a better school teacher than observer. If not, the future of America was doomed. "Kade and Cassie."

Like a comic strip in an old Sunday newspaper, Garret's eyes circled round, his jaw dropped slightly open and Rachel could almost see the light bulb turning on above his head.

"I'll be…" Preston followed everyone's gaze.

Carson burst out laughing. "Ten bucks says the marriage sticks."

"I'm in on that." his wife Jess smiled at him. "Just look at them."

"At what?" This time the obtuse one was Preston. "They're dancing. People dance all the time."

"My husband, the romantic." Sarah Sue sighed. "Honey, take a closer look. If they stood any closer, you wouldn't be able to slip a sheet of paper between them."

"And the way he's gazing into her eyes," Jackie added.

Jess chuckled. "Like she was a banana split with whipped cream and extra cherries on top."

This time Carson nodded. "Or a Napoleon brandy about to be uncorked."

"I think it's sweet." Jillian sat back, still watching the dancing couple as Kade slowly spun her around before pulling Cassie back into the circle of his arms. "No pun intended."

"You gotta admit, the fates seem to be on our side." Garret kept his eyes on the two dancing as well. "Five of us made marriage deals and five of us found the love of our lives. Our perfect soul mates."

"And it looks like fate has done it again," Rachel chimed in. "I'd bet the ranch those two are going to stay married."

"Don't go there," Preston teased, then laughed. "But I do agree. They've got that sparkle in their eyes, and frankly, they look about ready to self-combust."

"So no one's betting against?" Rachel asked.

All the heads at the table turned left then right.

"Do you think," Rachel shifted her attention from the

couple on the floor to the happily married couples at the table, "we'll ever tell Mom how the six of us wound up married?"

In complete choral unison, the voices at the table instantly echoed, "No!" then burst into laughter. Fate really did have an interesting sense of humor, didn't she?

CHAPTER THIRTEEN

Lunch was always a crapshoot at the Sweet Ranch. Some days the kitchen overflowed with siblings and now their spouses, other days the midday mealtime was quieter and less chaotic. Today was somewhere in the middle. Kade leaned against the counter, watching as his mother bustled between the stove and the table, refusing help from anyone who offered. He couldn't help but smile at Cassie who, ignoring his mother, was setting the table. Every time Alice Sweet told her to sit and relax, Cassie merely smiled and replied, "Yes, ma'am," then continued in search of silverware and plates while Rachel brought pitchers of tea and lemonade from the extra fridge.

At the table, Preston and Sarah Sue sat side by side, their heads together in a familiar private conversation that made him want to smile even wider. He loved how this family was growing. And a growing part of him wished he could be here more often.

"All right. That's it." His mom set a platter of leftover pork chops in front of his brother. The table was pretty much overflowing with a potluck of the week's family dinners—or what was left of them.

Chairs scraped against the floor. On either side of him, his sister and wife settled at the table. *Wife.* Not a word he was used to using. Oddly enough, it didn't sound as startling as he would have thought. As a matter of fact, it seemed to feel… right.

"Earth to Kade." From across the table, his mother waved her hand at him. "Are you planning on joining us today?"

"Oh," he shook his head, "sorry. Thinking."

"That's fine, but pass the potatoes while you're at it." Her tone was slightly scolding, but her smile softened the blow. It always had.

Sarah Sue glanced at the kitchen clock then out the window. "I wonder what's keeping Dad. I told him lunch would be a little late, after one, today, but…"

"I bet he lost track of time." Alice offered a reassuring smile. "I'll send him a quick reminder text."

Just as his mom pushed back from the table to retrieve her phone, Sarah Sue's handbag began to ring.

His mom laughed. "I bet he just noticed the time. I swear, for the best family doctor in this state, that man can be awfully absent-minded."

Sarah Sue hurried across, answered, nodded, grunted, mumbled, "I'll tell everyone," then closed her phone.

"Something wrong?" Worry etched across his mother's forehead.

"Dad can't make it. He's heading to the hospital. Emily Henderson is on her way to the ER."

"Oh," Alice tsked. "That poor family. Emily has had such a hard time of it the last few years. I'll be praying that whatever is wrong isn't serious."

"We all will," Rachel added.

Cassie leaned toward Kade. "Henderson… Is her brother the kid busing tables at the Whiskey Moon?"

"That would be him," Preston said.

She didn't say another word but Kade could almost read the thoughts in her mind as if they were printed on her forehead. He couldn't blame her, he was thinking the same thing—that kid had it rough enough right now. A sister in the hospital was probably the last thing he and his family needed.

The conversation drifted to other, less serious subjects. Kade ate, only half-listening, his mind sifting through his to-do list before leaving for temporary duty. After lunch, with the clanking of dishes and glasses filling the room as the table was cleared, he caught Cassidy's eye and gave a slight nod toward the back door. Though he shouldn't have been surprised that she immediately understood and excused herself to join him on the back porch, he wasn't. Everything about this business deal was beginning to feel more and more like anything but business.

"Since I'm not needed for any chores on the ranch, this afternoon would be a good time to run to the bank. Set up that account we discussed."

Her gaze to the floor, she blew out a deep sigh. "Your family is providing me with room and board. It doesn't feel right taking your money too."

"I won't be here much over the course of the coming year and life is unpredictable, you'll need to have access to money, just in case."

Her mouth clamped shut, her gaze steadied on a distant point, but she didn't say a word.

"Or would you rather ask Mom to lend you money if you need it?"

That had her head whipping around. "Of course not."

"Then we agree the account is practical?"

Another heavy sigh, and she nodded. "Okay. Maybe you have a point."

"That's my girl."

As soon as everything was cleaned up from lunch, the two of them headed to town. Kade pulled into an open space in front of the massive building that looked exactly like what it was—a bank. Taking hold of her hand, supposedly for appearances, he knew it was simply because that was what felt normal now.

Inside, one of the associates directed them to an open cubicle with a bank officer. Filling out the standard paperwork, they were almost done presenting identification and signing the account cards when a raised voice from the back of the lobby caught his attention.

The older man dressed in Friday business casual was coming out of another cubicle, chased by a younger man. Jacob Henderson.

"I've explained it all to your father," the older man spoke as he walked, his stride rapid, and aloof. "I really don't have time to discuss this with you, I'm late for an important meeting. Call my office number and we'll make an appointment for another day." The man didn't even bother to look back at the kid.

"Appointment?" Jacob's face flushed, not with embarrassment, or heat, but with pure unadulterated anger. "We're talking about my sister!" he shouted.

"You're upset. That's understandable." The man barely slowed his pace. "But I really need to go."

"We want our money." The words came out sharp, crisp, and laced with fury.

Riveted to the scene unfolding before him, Kade wondered who this guy was and why Jacob was so angry.

The man finally stopped and spun around to face the kid. "I've explained to your father—"

"I don't want to hear your excuses. You're nothing but a crook, and everyone needs to know it!"

Cassie's fingers dug into Kade's arm. "Uh-oh."

"What?" Kade tore his gaze away from the unfolding drama and looked where Cassie's eyes were glued to the young man and the one hand still in his pocket. *Aw, crap.* Just what they didn't need, a distraught unstable teen with a gun.

"Gun." Kade's voice was a tight whisper. His jaw clenched and she could see his military mind calculating distances, opportunities. If he found the moment to reach for his own gun, that poor kid would not walk out of here.

Still shouting at the man, Jacob's left hand gestured wildly, punctuating his words, but his right hand... his right hand remained jammed deep in the front pocket of his sweatshirt. It didn't move. People who were this agitated, this angry, used both hands. They pointed, they balled their fists. Jacob's stillness on one side was a glaring anomaly, a detail that was fundamentally wrong.

Cassidy's eyes narrowed, her focus absolute. She saw the way the fabric of that one pocket sagged, pulled down by something heavy and dense. It wasn't a phone. It wasn't a wallet. It didn't sway when he shifted his weight; it hung with a leaden, solid feel. He was angling his body, subconsciously shielding that side of himself, protecting it. The world narrowed to the space between the bank officer's desk and the front door.

Kade's body remained rigid beside her; she knew he was waiting for the right moment to pounce. Save the day. Her knight in shining armor.

The scene unfolded in a series of sharp, terrifying snapshots. Jacob Henderson, the tired, hard-working kid from the hardware store, was standing in the middle of the bank lobby, his face pale and tear-streaked, fury oozing from every pore. Worse still, she saw desperation in his eyes. She'd seen it a thousand times or more in the eyes of people who had gambled away everything they owned, and sometimes more. This was not looking good. Not at all.

"You're upset." The banker's voice was deliberately calm, and clearly patronizing. "I understand, but making a scene isn't going to help anyone."

"Help anyone?" Jacob's voice cracked. "My sister is in the hospital. They're taking her to the ICU. The ICU!" he repeated. "None of this would have happened if she'd had the surgery. You promised my father."

Cassie was struggling to put the pieces together. What did this man have to do with Emily going to the hospital?

The other customers in the bank had gone quiet, watching the emotional scene unfold like a made-for-TV movie. Eyes wide, a teller behind the counter whispered to another, the bank officer who'd been helping them slowly closed the folder containing their paperwork.

"Where's security?" Cassie whispered, leaning against Kade.

"Small town," he murmured back, his gaze fixed on Jacob. "No one thinks they need paid security. Not even a bank."

The bank man was backing away, hands raised slightly. "Listen, young man, the market has risks. I told your father that. Nothing is guaranteed—"

"You said it was safe!" Jacob's hand remained in his

pocket. "You said you could double, maybe even triple our savings." His eyes filled with unshed tears at the same time his jaw clenched, turning the pain to fury once again. "You promised."

Cassie watched Jacob carefully. The dark circles under his eyes had deepened since she'd seen him at the Whiskey Moon. No sleep, a sick sister, and a loaded gun topped with a heavy dose of desperation were a very deadly cocktail.

"One of the lease holders defaulted. It happens. All the time. It's no big deal." The man's voice was laced with impatience now. "It's unfortunate timing, but if you just wait, the investment will likely recover—"

"Wait?" Jacob's voice rose an octave. "Emily can't wait. She needs that surgery now."

The irritated man shook his head. "You should be having this argument with your insurance company, not me."

Aw hell, Cassie thought. Pass the buck, just what this kid didn't need to hear. And then it happened. Jacob's hand slid out of his pocket, a semi-automatic handgun clenched tightly in his fingers.

"Put that thing away before someone gets hurt." The man's voice took on a dismissive tone. "This isn't a video game, kid."

Cassie rolled her eyes. Kade's hands rolled into a fist. They both recognized this guy was clearly an idiot, beautifully skilled at making things worse.

Jacob lifted his arm, his gaze shifting to the front door. The crack of the gunshot was deafening—and terrifying.

A flower pot exploded in a shower of terracotta and dirt. The woman who had been at the teller window screamed a high, thin sound of pure panic. People instantly dropped to the floor, a few scrambling on all fours for cover. Pulling Cassie out of her seat, Kade had her smothered in his grip, his body molded around hers, shielding her from any more flying bullets. She could feel the frantic hammering of his heart against her back.

"I know this isn't a game. Do you?" The torment in Jacob's voice and gaze had shifted to something hard as steel and even more dangerous.

The bank man's eyes widened and Cassie wouldn't be at all surprised if he had just soiled his pants.

"Not such a big shot now, are you?" Jacob's anger was definitely escalating. He was losing his grip on reality.

From her position on the floor, Cassie scanned her surroundings, taking note of every tiny detail, all the while praying Kade didn't go into warrior mode. Crouched behind her desk, the branch manager's hand reached slowly toward something beneath—an alarm, no doubt. Smart. But it also meant the police would be on their way, a complication that could make everything a hundred times worse. Despite how dangerous all of this was, how badly it could turn out, her heart still ached for the frustrated, hurt and desperately misguided teen.

"You," Jacob practically growled at the man, the gun trained on him. "You're going to fix this."

Shaking his head, the man raised his hands, as if that would save him from being torn apart by a bullet like the shattered pot. "Jacob, please, I can't just—"

"I want our money back."

"It doesn't work that way. You know that. Your father knows that. It's only a paper loss. As I said before, in time you'll get your money back."

"Time? Emily doesn't have time!"

Cassie could feel Kade's body coiled like a spring ready to launch. She'd come to know him well enough to understand he wasn't the kind of man to sit back and do nothing. On top of that, with his military training, he most likely was waiting for an opening, ready to tackle the boy, even shoot him if necessary. And deep in her gut, she knew he would risk his own life if it meant saving another.

She'd also worked with enough desperate gamblers to understand what was happening under the surface. Jacob wasn't a criminal; he was a terrified kid watching his sister suffer, believing this man was responsible. He didn't want to hurt anyone else—she had to believe that—he only wanted this man to do the right thing. The problem, of course, as far as she could tell, there wasn't a damn thing this guy could do, besides make things worse. Especially if he kept opening his mouth.

Having calculated the risks, the potential outcomes, the response time for a small-town police force, taking a deep breath, she inched out of Kade's grip, quickly shoving to her feet before he could stop her. Kade could tackle him, but she had to try talking this kid off the ledge first, she had to.

On her feet, hands up, her gaze met Jacob's. The only sound in the cavernous lobby was a still small voice. Kade's whispering, "Oh, hell."

CHAPTER FOURTEEN

The world condensed to a single, terrifying point: Cassidy, standing.

Kade's every instinct screamed at him to move, to pull her back, to put himself between her and the trembling barrel of that gun. He was a soldier. His body was trained for this, hardwired to neutralize a threat, to protect. But he was frozen, his hand still outstretched from where she had slipped from his grasp. Any sudden movement from him, any aggressive action, and he knew Jacob's panic could erupt into a tragedy that no one in this room would ever walk away from. He could only watch. It was the most profound form of helplessness he had ever known.

"Jacob," Cassidy's voice cut through the ringing silence. It was calm. Impossibly, unbelievably calm. She didn't shout. She didn't plead. She just spoke, her tone even and steady, as if they were the only two people in the room. "My name is Cassie. We met the other day. At the hardware store."

Jacob's wild, terrified eyes focused on her.

Kade's heart slammed against his ribs. The gun was now pointed at his wife—his Cassie—and there were fifteen feet of open space between them. Too far to reach her in time if Jacob's finger tightened on that trigger, and from where he was, even if he could retrieve his gun quickly, he simply didn't have a kill shot, Cassie was in the way.

"I just want to talk," Cassie continued, her voice remaining calm. "You must be tired. Would you like to sit down?"

The kid frowned and Kade would give anything to know exactly what he was thinking. "No," he finally muttered.

"Okay." Cassie stood perfectly still. "Have you had anything to eat today?"

Again, Jacob's gaze narrowed before he once again shook his head.

"Are you hungry? I'm sure we can get some food sent in for you."

"No." This time there was no hesitation.

Cassie bobbed her head. "I heard about your sister Emily. I'm so, so sorry. I can't imagine how scared you must be right now."

His wife shifted slightly to her right and ignoring how his heart hammered against his ribs, he reassessed angles, recalculated the number of steps it would take to disarm the kid, weighed the risk of a ricochet off the marble floor. The risks were still too damn high. The one person he wanted to save more than anything, was the one most likely to get hurt—or killed. *Damn it.*

"You don't know anything about it." Jacob's voice seemed to thicken with emotion, his anger slipping.

"You're right, I don't," she said, her voice softening even more. "But I know what it's like to feel like the whole world is against you. To feel like you have to do something, anything, to fix a problem that's just too big." She took a single, slow, deliberate step to the side, moving slightly away from the rest of the huddled group, drawing Jacob's focus entirely onto her. It was a tactical move, one Kade recognized with a jolt of astonishment. She was isolating the threat.

"You're just trying to help your sister." It wasn't a question. It was a statement of fact, an acknowledgment of his motive that seemed to momentarily drain even more anger from his posture.

Her focus was entirely on Jacob. "This is a bad situation. But it doesn't have to get worse." She waved her hand to the huddled group of innocent bystanders. "What do you say if we let these other people go? They haven't done anything, have they?"

Without hesitation the kid shook his head, then scanned

the people as if only now realizing he and this idiot weren't alone.

"Can we let them go?"

For just a split second, Kade thought he was going to agree, and then his back snapped straight and he shook his head. "No."

"Okay." Cassie nodded. "That's okay if that makes you feel better. Do you feel better?"

Again, the kid hesitated, considering her words. Kade watched, mesmerized. She was actually connecting with this kid.

The kid's gaze met hers. "I'll feel better when Emily is better."

"Of course you will." Cassie's stance remained calm, casual. "You love your sister."

The kid just nodded. What Kade couldn't decide was if they were making progress or not. He was, however, extremely grateful that the banking idiot who started this whole mess was clearly too petrified to open his mouth.

"That's a nice bracelet," her voice remained impossibly calm. "Did you make it?"

The question was so absurd, so completely out of left field that it had Jacob's head snapping back before looking down at the worn leather bracelet on his wrist. "My sister did," he mumbled, his voice barely a whisper. "For my birthday."

"It's beautiful." Cassidy smiled ever so sweetly. "She's very talented."

Kade could feel the shift in the room. The air was still thick with terror, but something else was creeping in. A thread of human connection, spun from a simple, unexpected question. He was still coiled, still ready to move, but a part of his soldier's brain watched her work with a sense of profound, disbelieving awe. He was trained to end a fight. She was trying to prevent one from ever truly starting. He could only pray she didn't get herself killed in the process.

"Jacob." Her voice was a soft, gentle murmur. "I know you're trying to be strong for her. But you can't help her from inside a jail cell. Let us help you. Let me help you."

Any fool could see the conflict in the boy's eyes, the war between desperation and the flicker of hope she was offering. The gun lowered, just an inch.

And then, in the distance, came the first, faint wail of an approaching siren. Jacob's head snapped up, his eyes wide with fresh panic, the gun coming back up, trembling more violently than before.

"Listen, Jacob." Cassie dared to take a step closer. "We don't have much time. If you put the gun down now, before anyone else arrives, this can still be fixed."

"Fixed how?" Suspicion crept back into his voice. "You can't fix this."

"Maybe not alone." Still blocking a shot, she glanced briefly at Kade, then back to Jacob. "But the Sweet family has lived here for generations, they have connections. Resources. Let us help you and Emily."

The gun wavered in Jacob's hand. "Why would you help us?"

"Because it's the right thing to do," Cassie said simply. "Because Emily deserves a chance. Because you deserve a chance."

The siren grew louder. Jacob's eyes darted toward the door, then back to Cassie. Panic flashed across his face. "They're coming for me," he whispered.

"Yes," Cassie didn't lie. "But what happens next is up to you."

"It's no use," Jacob muttered, his arm straightening, the gun pointed directly and firmly at Cassie.

In that very instant, Kade knew the minute the doors flew open and the police barged in, that terrified kid was going to pull the trigger and there wasn't a damn thing Kade could do about it.

Cassidy's breath hitched, every muscle in her body screamed at her to dive for cover. A perfect dark circle, a tiny terrifying void, the barrel of the gun was aimed directly at the center of her chest. And yet, she didn't move. Her gaze was locked with Jacob's. His eyes didn't reflect a killer's rage, but a cornered animal's pure, abject terror. The sirens were closer now, their wails a rising, frantic scream.

Time seemed to slow, to stretch. Like a movie scene suddenly rolling in slow motion. Everything came into strange, hyper-focused clarity: the frantic pounding of her own heart; the glint of the fluorescent lights on the gun's slide; and Kade, a coiled, powerful presence only yards away, ready to launch himself into the path of a bullet meant for her. With a certainty as absolute as the gun in Jacob's hand, she knew she could not let that happen.

"Jacob," she didn't dare move, "do you know what Emily would say if she could see you right now?"

The question hung in the air between them. His eyes flickered with uncertainty. "She'd be scared," he whispered finally. "Scared for me."

"Yes, she would." Cassie took a small, careful step forward. "She wouldn't want this for you." The sirens were louder now, maybe a block away. She had seconds, not minutes.

"I can't face her if I've failed." Jacob's voice cracked.

"You haven't failed her." Cassie held his gaze. "Loving someone enough to risk everything for them—that's never failure."

His arm trembled, the gun wavering slightly.

"Emily needs her big brother," she continued. "Not a memory, not a story about what happened to him. She needs you there, beside her, holding her hand. Every step of the way."

The shrill, jarring ring of a telephone cut through the tension. It was the landline on the bank officer's desk. It rang once. Twice. From outside, a new sound boomed through the thick glass of the bank doors. "Jacob Henderson, this is Sheriff Brody. Pick up the phone. Let's talk about this."

Jacob flinched, his head snapping toward the sound, his wild eyes darting between the door and the ringing phone.

The gun wavered. This was the moment. He was losing control, caught between the external threat of the police and the internal storm of his own desperation.

"Jacob, look at me." Cassidy's voice cut through his panic, pulling his focus back to her. "The sheriff is a good man. He just wants to talk." She took a single, slow step forward, making herself the sole focus. A tactical move. "You should answer it."

"They'll arrest me," he whispered, his voice cracking.

"Yes." She nodded. If she understood one thing about negotiating, it was that she could not lie to him. Could not risk losing his trust. "They will. But what happens after that… we can work on that. Together. I promised I would help you, and I will. My husband," the word felt solid, real on her tongue, "is a Sergeant First Class in the United States Army. He'll help. His family will help. They know lawyers. Good lawyers." Oh, how she hoped she wasn't lying. "And if you let me have that gun, he'll make sure when the police come inside, they won't hurt you. It's the only way, Jacob. One step at a time."

She saw the flicker of comprehension, the dawning realization of the forces arrayed against him.

"You have to put the gun down. Now." She took a chance and extended her arm, palm open and up.

Nothing. At least he wasn't pulling the trigger.

"Jacob. It's the only way to help Emily. Do this for Emily."

It was his sister's name that did it. A ragged sob tore from his throat. Something in his face crumpled. The gun lowered, inch by inch. "I don't know what to do," he mumbled.

"Give me the gun," she repeated. "And we'll tell the police it's over."

For one breathless moment, the world balanced on a knife's edge. Then, with a broken sob, Jacob placed the weapon in her outstretched palm. "I'm sorry," he sobbed. "I'm so sorry."

Relief flooded through her. Extending her arm, she glanced at Kade. No words were needed. As Jacob fell into her arms sobbing, no longer an angry threat but a broken child, Kade took the gun, engaged the safety, set it on a desk far from people, and opened the doors to the street.

"It will be okay," she murmured to the still sobbing teen.

Quickly, the sheriff and his officers came to her side, each one assessing the situation. "Anyone wounded?"

"No," Cassie answered. "No, we're all fine."

Glancing around, the sheriff seemed confused. It took a moment for him to realize that the sobbing teen wasn't a scared victim but the perpetrator of today's hostage crisis. "Come with me, son."

Jacob lifted his head from Cassie's shoulder. Tired, questioning eyes met hers.

"Go on. It will be all right. You'll see."

Hands cuffed behind him, an officer escorted Jacob to a squad car while the EMTs tended to a profusely sweating investment banker. And Kade appeared at her side, his arms wrapping around her, his face buried in her hair. She clung to him, the scent of him—coffee, soap, and something uniquely Kade—filling her senses. They stood like that for a long, silent moment.

When he finally pulled back, his hands came up to frame her face, his thumbs gently brushing at her cheek. His eyes, a raw storm of emotion—relief, fear, and something so powerful it stole the breath from her lungs. "Don't you ever do that to me again."

"I'll try not to make a habit of it." She actually chuckled.

Shaking his head, the slightest of smiles touched his lips. "What am I going to do with you?" He leaned his forehead against hers, his own breath shaky. "All I could think, over and over on a never-ending loop, was what would I do without you."

The confession, torn from him in the raw aftermath of terror, was the most beautiful thing she had ever heard. "Thank you."

"Thank you?"

"For caring."

Now he laughed. Not a hilarious how funny are you laugh, but more of a you've got to be kidding laugh. "Caring. Oh, Cassie. I don't care about you, I love you. As in the till death do us part kind of love."

"You… what?" She knew she was probably gaping like a landed trout.

His smile softened. "I love you, Mrs. Sweet. With everything in me. And if you're willing, I'd like to see if maybe we can't renegotiate our little deal."

Her heart was racing faster than a thoroughbred at the Derby. Could this all be a dream? Maybe any minute she was going to wake up and discover there was no hostage situation, no frazzled teen, no gun, no police, and no renegotiations. Because right about now, she couldn't think of anything she wanted more than to renegotiate. "Would it help—in the negotiations, that is—if I told you that I love you?"

A smile as wide as the Rio Grande took over his face. "What do you say we go home and find out?"

CHAPTER FIFTEEN

The older Kade got, the earlier mornings seemed to roll around, and the harder getting out of bed seemed to be. Glancing at the clock on the nightstand, he saw that it was almost five am. Maybe he could steal a few more minutes with his wife. Rolling over, his arm instinctively went to wrap around Cassie, something that had become a morning ritual since that day at the bank, and since they agreed to make this marriage work for real. Not that there was much work involved, loving Cassie was crazy easy. That is when she was here. His eyes sprang open, staring at the empty bed beside him. Where the heck had she gone at this hour?

Showered and dressed, he made his way downstairs in search of his wife. He found his mother at the stove, cooking breakfast the same as she always did, but no sign of Cassie.

"She's in the barn." His mother didn't look at him, but he could see her wide smile.

"The barn?"

"Yeah," she turned to face him, waving a fork, "that big building with a hay loft and animals by the paddock."

"Ha ha," he teased, pouring himself a travel mug of coffee. "Why is she in the barn?"

"Clint mentioned the mare is having a hard labor. Since I can handle breakfast on my own, she went out there to deal with the mare." Putting a lid on the pan, she turned to her son. "She fits."

Kade raised his brows at his mom.

"Don't look at me like that. I love all my children-in-law, but she's different. She seems to have been born to be a rancher, which, if I might say, is darn unusual for a city girl."

He'd thought that himself, and he'd noticed almost since the day they'd arrived. She'd taken to everything from the dirty work of mucking stalls, to the hard work of digging fence posts, to the crazy early hours, and everything else in between. He would have loved her regardless, but her love of the ranch life made his heart swell. "She's definitely a natural."

"I'll tell you something else."

Kade nodded.

"Your dad would be dang pleased to know that there's someone in this next generation who loves ranching."

He couldn't help the smile that teased at the corners of his mouth. "Dad would love her." And he was pretty sure, Cassie would have loved his father.

"You're thinking about the future, aren't you? Funny how time, and the right person, can change what we thought we wanted out of life." His mom went back to flipping bacon.

All he did was nod. He had to talk to Cassidy before he made any decisions. It was something new for him, not just doing whatever he thought was appropriate. Having to consider someone else's thoughts and feelings, but he loved it. More than he'd ever thought he could. "Has she had her tea?"

His mom shook her head. "She headed out before the water boiled."

Taking another couple of minutes, he poured her tea the way he knew she liked it. Putting a lid on the mug, and kissing his mom on the forehead, headed to the barn.

Once he reached the open doors, he could hear Cassie speaking ever so softly, offering words of comfort to the tired first time mare. Following the sound of her voice to the oversized foaling stall in the back of the barn, he came to a stop short of the gate, but able to see everything.

The mare, one of their best quarter horses, was lying on her side in a deep bed of clean straw, her dark coat slick with sweat. Her sides heaved with a ragged, uneven rhythm, and a low, guttural groan rumbled from deep in her chest. Clint stood just outside the stall, his arms leaning on the gate, his expression a mask of professional, worried patience. But it was Cassidy who held Kade's focus. She was in the stall with the mare, kneeling in the straw near the animal's head, one hand resting gently on the mare's neck, her thumb drawing slow, steady circles against the damp hide. Her head was bowed close to the horse's, and her voice was a low, continuous murmur, a soft, melodic stream of nonsense and reassurance that was the only sound in the stall besides the mare's labored breathing. She wasn't a vet or a ranch hand in that moment; she was a calm, steady anchor in a storm of pain and fear. Much like she'd been not long ago for Jacob. This woman was a gift of comfort and peace.

The mare's muscles bunched for another unproductive contraction. The horse lifted its head, a flicker of panic in its wide, dark eyes. Cassie didn't flinch. She just kept stroking, her voice never wavering. "It's okay, mama," she whispered, the words carrying across the quiet barn. "You're okay. You can do this." She leaned in, humming a simple, repetitive tune, a sound so full of gentle empathy that would have soothed the most agitated of beasts.

Hands hanging over the low fence, Clint nodded slowly, a look of profound respect on the new foreman's weathered face. The seasoned cowboy knew exactly what he was seeing: a quiet miracle of instinct and compassion at work.

Kade unlatched the gate and strolled inside. Sitting beside his wife, he handed her the cup of tea, stroking the mare's neck so his wife could enjoy her morning brew.

"Thank you." Her smile bloomed and after the first sip, she heaved a contented sigh. "I really needed that."

"Glad to help." They sat together, Cassie stroking the horse, Kade gently rubbing her shoulder with his free hand. Was there anything more peaceful than love and Mother Nature? "I need to talk to you about something."

Her gaze shifted to his, a sudden spark of concern in her eyes.

"Nothing bad." He raised one hand palm out. "But you

know I have to leave for my new assignment soon, and yes, I'll be close enough to come home here and there, but it's got me thinking."

She nodded, her gaze shifting from the horse to Clint and back.

The foreman took a step into the stall. "I'd say you've done a good job of calming our girl down." He took a moment to examine the mare and nodded. "Yep. It won't be long now. If you two want to head back to the house and get your breakfast, I'll call if we need you again."

Cassie hesitated before nodding, and pushing to her feet.

He loved how much she cared about everything to do with the ranch and the animals. His heart had never been so happy.

Cassie tried not to fear the worst. She'd never been an optimist, but not a pessimist either, just a matter of fact. But that was before she cared so much, and she cared more than she'd ever cared about anything when it came to Kade and his family. "Is something wrong?"

He shook his head. "No, but come with me." He redirected her into the tack room where Preston had a small desk set up and reached for a cardboard tube. "I've been thinking a lot about life—our life—and where we're going."

She nodded. They'd had snippets of this conversation. Knew that he was questioning his life plans now that he had a wife.

"I really thought I would stay in Uncle Sam's army until he threw me out."

Again, she nodded, not saying a word, just listening.

"I don't want to do that anymore."

The whole time she'd known him, from what he'd said now and then, it was pretty clear that his career in the army seemed to mean so much to him. "Are you sure?"

"Very." He pulled papers out of the tube and opened

them on the desk, taking a couple of leather weights to hold it open. "I have no choice but to finish this TDY and another year, then I can retire with my twenty."

She knew he was close to qualifying for retirement and a pension, though the idea of retiring in your thirties was rather foreign to her.

"After that, I'd like to come work the ranch. All of my siblings have careers. Yes, they help with the ranch, we've proven we can all work together to run the place, but this isn't their dream."

"But it is yours?" Working with him, she'd noticed a different level of satisfaction in Kade than when she worked with any of his siblings. He was right, they loved the ranch, but working it day after day wasn't in them.

His head bobbed. "And I think yours."

She couldn't stop the smile that took over her face. Everything any foster kid had ever dreamed of was here at the ranch. The family, the love, the camaraderie, the land and the animals, all of it gave her more grounding than any college degree, or fancy job in a big city.

"Thought so." His smile widened. "So, Carson introduced me to a buddy of his. This house is Mom's. It's her home, but eventually, it will be more than even she needs."

Cassie nibbled on her lower lip, not sure where he was going with this.

"Don't worry. I chatted with Mom first." He sighed. "Maybe I should have told you first, but I thought, if Mom wasn't in agreement, there was no point."

"Okay..." It made sense. Her gaze followed his fingers on the papers—blueprints, actually.

"This here is the main house. And this," his finger moved, "is a mother-in-law suite. Two bedrooms, two and a half baths, small living, kitchen and dining."

"You want your mother to live there?" She didn't understand, he just said this big old house was her home.

"Not yet."

Now she lifted her gaze to meet his. She wasn't following.

"I thought we could live here once I'm fully separated from Uncle Sam. You can make any changes you want, we'd have our own private place, but be close enough to the hub of the family and the house. Then, when the time was right, we'd swap."

Her gaze returned to the plans. A cozy cottage-like home attached to the main house, just the right size for a couple. Her mind looked more closely. Every single line and drawing seemed…perfect. And then, some day, they'd raise a family in the big house.

His finger hooked under her chin and lifted her face to his. "You're blushing. Do you not like this idea? You can tell me. It's okay, we can come up with a new plan."

She shook her head and grabbed hold of his hand. "I think it's a fantastic idea."

"For now, while I'm gone, you'd stay in the big house with everyone. Unless you want to move sooner."

"No. I love that big house and being so close to everyone."

His head tipped to one side. "Why were you blushing?"

Her gaze falling to the paper, she felt her cheeks warm again. "I guess I was thinking about a family." She lifted her face and leveled her eyes with his. "Ours."

Relief washed over her as his smile grew even wider. "I like the sound of that. Our family."

"Me too."

Pulling her around to fully face him, he curled her against him, his face dipping until his mouth found hers for a soul stealing kiss that made her toes curl and her heart hammer fast and hard. Oh, how she loved this man.

Forever never sounded so good.

EPILOGUE

The way Kade and Cassie were attached at the hip, anyone would think he would be returning to active duty on the other side of the world and not the state of Texas. Even Brady had once again abandoned Alice to lie at his master's feet.

"They look good." Alice's sister Vicki came to stand at her side.

"They all look so happy. Reminds me of Charlie and me."

"Yeah," Vicki agreed. "You two were one heck of a match."

Some days, Alice could swear Charlie was standing at her side, smiling as their family grew. Other days, she'd completely forgotten what it was like to live and work at his side. It shouldn't be like that. Charlie was the love of her life and she should feel him in her heart every second of every day, but he seemed to be slipping away.

"Ever ask yourself why those two stayed married?"

The million-dollar question. With an easy answer. "For the money."

Vicki eased back her gaze shifting from Kade and Cassie on the back porch swing, hands threaded together, her head on his shoulder, and enough love oozing to shower the entire great state of Texas. "Money?"

"The trust."

"Oh." Vicki returned her attention to the couple simply enjoying sitting side by side. "So he drank too much, married a stranger, and decided to stay married for the money, and just happened to fall in love?"

"Yeah." Alice smiled. "That pretty much covers it."

"They told you that?"

"Of course not. None of them did."

"None of them?" Now Vicki's eyes were practically falling out of her head.

Chuckling, Alice put her hand on her sister's arm. "Come on, Vick. Six kids, six sudden marriages, and a sudden river of money to save the ranch. Really?"

"You're sure?"

"Positive."

"But they all look so in love." Her sister's gaze shifted across the yard to all her nieces and nephews. From the croquet that had Preston and Sarah teamed up against Carson and Jess in a heated match that had each couple slapping high fives and swapping quick intimate kisses. Over to Garret and Jackie playing corn hole with Rachel and Jim and Jillian and Blake. All of them stealing kisses and hugs as if they were besotted teens with their first love. And of course, Kade and Cassie who hadn't moved off that swing for hours. Just watching the family welcome home barbecue unfold before them.

"That's because they are." Alice rocked on her toes and bit back a huge smile. She never would have agreed to such a plan, but since her children thought it worth trying to pull the wool over her eyes, the least she could do was play along. Especially since in each case cupid's arrow had struck. "You know what they say: life is what happens while you're busy making other plans."

"I don't know. One couple maybe. But six? No. I vote for love at first sight and happily ever after."

Alice certainly wasn't going to argue the happily ever after, and maybe there had even been a little love at first sight. No matter how it played out though, her family was happy, and growing and she was sure Charlie was smiling down on them all from heaven. She'd actually asked herself a time or two if maybe Charlie had somehow had something to do with all these perfect matches. Then again, she was probably being silly. All that mattered is that everyone was happy. And maybe, soon, she'd have a yard full of her kids' kids running and playing. Yep, she could hardly wait to see what else life had in store for all of them.

MEET CHRIS

USA TODAY Bestselling Author of dozens of contemporary novels, including the award winning Aloha Series, Chris Keniston lives in suburban Dallas with her husband, two human children, and two canine children. Though she loves her puppies equally, she admits being especially attached to her German Shepherd rescue. After all, even dogs deserve a happily ever after.

More on Chris and all her books can be found at
www.chriskeniston.com

Follow Chris' Monday Blog at her website
ChrisKenistonAuthor

Follow Chris on Facebook at
ChrisKenistonAuthor

Never miss a New Release!
Sign up for News from Chris:
www.chriskeniston.com/newsletter.html

Questions? Comments?
I would love to hear from you! You can reach me at:
chris@chriskeniston.com